Hot Fudge

S T O R I E S

Richard Spilman

P O S E I D O N   P R E S S

NEW YORK   LONDON   TORONTO   SYDNEY   TOKYO

Poseidon Press
Simon & Schuster Building
Rockefeller Center
1230 Avenue of the Americas
New York, New York 10020

POSEIDON PRESS is a registered trademark
of Simon & Schuster Inc.

POSEIDON PRESS colophon is a trademark
of Simon & Schuster Inc.

Designed by Karolina Harris
Manufactured in the United States of America

1   3   5   7   9   10   8   6   4   2

Library of Congress Cataloging-in-Publication Data

Spilman, Richard.
Hot fudge: stories/Richard Spilman.
p.   cm.
I.   Title.
PS3569.P5435H6   1990
813'.54—dc20   89-29618
CIP

ISBN 0-671-68544-9

To Roy and Evelyn Spilman

CONTENTS

The Old Man
Tells His Story
and Gets It Wrong

THEY sat in the shadow of the house. Bright sunlight hurt the old man's eyes—even from the shade he could not look into the yard without squinting. They sat in redwood chairs on a lawn speckled with daisies and dandelions, and as Carl talked, his chair rocked on two legs. Three empty beer bottles stood on a small bench between them. His daughter had gone, assuring him that she would be back soon. He tried to remember where she went but gave up, afraid he would lose track of what the boy was saying. His grandson had returned from summer ROTC camp and was full of wonders—rifles that found their targets in the dark and tiny round grenades with a range so wide they'd kill the man who threw them carelessly—which fascinated the old man and brought back memories of the War. He rubbed his hands, which were cold despite the nearly smothering late spring heat, and his eyes wandered from the bed of withered daffodils to the line of buttonbush along the fence, wrapped in flowering honeysuckle, into the oak above them, whose branches spread over the entire house. He heard explosions and rifle fire and, from the tree, the cries of hundreds of birds.

With a sound like the creaking of canvas, the chair rocked back and forth, pushed by a bare foot in a torn sneaker, while the boy's pale voice described blast holes and shivered targets. Still no meat on him, his grandfather thought.

The old man hated to be alone with strangers, and over the last few months almost everyone but the daughter he lived with had become a stranger, even Carl. Sooner or later he'd lose track of the conversation. There would be silence, the two of them smiling the way people do when they can't understand each other's language, and the old man would feel called upon to apologize. "I ain't what I used to be," as if he had ever known what he used to be.

"The last night was a real trip," the boy enthused. "E and E—Escape and Evasion. They take you out at night and drop you in the middle of nowhere and leave you to find your way back. The seniors play the enemy. If they catch you, you're dead."

All your life, his grandfather thought. Escape and Evasion. His father, his wife, the banks, the lawyers, the Germans—he'd fought them when he could, and when he couldn't, he had run away. Most of the time it was useless, and some of the time it was wrong, but even when he had hated himself, it had felt good to fight. Imprisoned now in a body that would not obey, he envied the boy's ability to do things he might regret.

A breeze rippled across the grass, through the swaying shadow of the oak. He barely felt it.

Senility, if it appeared, would come upon him gradually, he'd thought, an enemy he could recognize and confront—but it hadn't. After a weekend of storms, he had gone out on the river in his boat. A flood had washed out one end of the dam across Sumner Creek, and bass had swum upriver to feed on the shad that came through the breach. Where the rough water smoothed into a current, there were underwater stumps. Casting among them, he began to feel as if the water were glass, a thick murky glass that his lure skidded across, and the men fishing from the bank and the clouds moving above them were slowly hardening into glass. Dark shapes moved beneath the surface, and he was afraid that any second they might break through. The fear took such a hold on him that he had to stop. But when he turned the boat, the brush along the creek seemed to merge into a solid mass. In a panic he tried to force his way through and grounded the boat on a bar. Someone had to wade out from shore to help.

High blood pressure, the doctors agreed, and something to do with valves. They gave him pills, but the confusion did not go away. It lay in the shadows of his mind

like a whisper at the bottom of a gravel pit. If he listened,
even for a second, he'd forget where he was.

"No compass, no map, no nothing. And it got cold at
night. I was the only one in my unit who had the sense to
bring a jacket. The guys called me a pussy, but they call
anyone a pussy who doesn't pretend he's got iron balls. I
told them, if there's a war it'll be the guys who don't
pretend who'll make it through."

The old man harrumphed, remembering the bodies
lying like busted grain sacks in a field of new wheat and
later, in occupied Germany, pictures of the dust and
gravel that had once been Hiroshima. Go ahead, he
thought, wear your jacket.

From this, he fell into mourning how quickly a man
disappeared in his children. In his prime, people had told
him he looked like Humphrey Bogart, and though his
back had stiffened he could still carry an eighty-pound
sack of cement from the truck to the garage. Yet across
from him sat a thin, blond, gangling creature, who had to
use both hands to lift a chair, and this was his grandson.
Two generations and what was left? Blue eyes, a crooked
smile, and long-fingered hands—the rest swallowed up in
others. He studied his own hands, which were swollen at
the knuckles, the age-spotted skin so papery he could
flake it off with a fingernail like the scales of a fish, and
glowered at the boy as if he had stolen something.

Once they'd almost gotten killed, the boy was saying,
because a couple of smart-asses had taken a shortcut
across a moonlit slash of open ground. For an hour they'd
had to lie in stinking mud at the edge of a slough and
listen to the underbrush crackling around them.

The smell of ripe silage rose in his grandfather's memory from the marsh he had slogged through the day his
regiment had parachuted into France. He was tempted to
tell the boy, but it would turn into a story, and that would
be too much trouble. His daughter would raise hell. You

never *talk* to people, she complained, you just tell them stories. The next thing I know, you'll be peeing in your pants.

There was no way to explain how it felt to live with nerves that would spin into nightmare at the backfire of a truck, in a world where a flash of light could make him anxious for hours and where he often couldn't walk around the block without losing his way. So how could he describe the joy of telling a story from beginning to end, feeling it draw him on and the pieces fall into place as they had seemed to do when his mind was whole? All his daughter heard was an old man repeating himself.

Anyway, it was a story to tell among men, that one. A woman wouldn't listen to killing, but if you said to a man, "I was scared, I was mad, I wanted to kill them, and when I did, it felt good," he'd hear you out. He knew what you were talking about.

Carl's chair thumped down, startling him, and he found himself face to face with his own crooked smile.

"I'm going to get another beer. Do you want one?"

The old man shook his head, thinking that if he followed the boy into the house, he could turn on the TV and they'd have an excuse not to talk. But it was afternoon—the soap operas were on. He couldn't watch soap operas, their plots jumped around too much. Through the glass of the patio door, he watched the boy's vague form moving in the kitchen. The heat felt as solid as a gag in his mouth.

He tried to imagine rifles that find their targets in the dark but couldn't. It seemed to be in the nature of things nowadays that he couldn't comprehend them. In the old world, his world, things acted the way everybody but a damned fool supposed they would. You could depend on them. Which was not to say that accidents didn't happen, but even the accidents were solid—the bank went under, the girl got pregnant, the crop failed—and you grew around them like the roots of a tree around a rock. Now the girls had pills and the farmers had insurance, and there were atoms and the insides of atoms and the insides of the insides (the boy had once tried to explain them to him.). He felt a kind of pity for the boy and for himself, because he was an old man, gone frail in infuriating ways, and because the world had gone feeble, too. And because the boy probably liked it that way.

His grandson stepped through the sliding glass door and pranced across the patio singing:

> You've got yoga, honey
> I've got beer
> You got overpriced
> And I got weird
> But it's all right. . . .

He plucked the empty bottle from the bench. "You sure you don't want another? I won't tell." And flipped it high, end over end, toward the trash barrels behind the garage. It landed with a *whang* that rolled through the old man like a scream.

"Goddamn you!" The glare leapt from the garden and burned all around him.

"Missed." Carl plopped into his chair. "What's wrong?"

His grandfather waited, trembling. The light slowly retreated. A cloud of images settled within him like sparks from a disturbed fire, dying before he could tell what they were. His stomach hurt.

"Did I scare you?"

"I've been scared since the day I was born," he said wearily. Then, realizing this was a confession of sorts, he added, "The Army gave me a medal for it."

"For being scared?"

"For running." *Stuck in a hedge, a muddy parachute strained one way, then another, in the wind.*

Carl ran a hand through his mare's nest of yellow hair. "You okay?"

The question was so transparent he had to laugh out loud. "Hell, no, I'm not okay. But there's nothing you can do about it."

"Mom says you're better."

"Your ma doesn't know her ass from a hole in the ground."

Carl sipped his beer and gazed down the line of hedges and fences where the backyards joined. "I wonder what I'd do if the bullets were real."

"The last thing you'd expect to do, probably." *The jig-saw of fields lay below him, beautiful and strange, and he could feel himself falling.* "They say you get used to fear, but you don't. You stumble along, shooting at people you can't see and wondering where the hell the war is. Then, right about the time you think you're not scared anymore, some poor bastard steps on a lump of loose dirt, and there it is. Like a wall."

"What did they give you the medal for?"

"Machine-gun nest. I must have told you that story."

"I think you tried to once, but Mom wouldn't let you."

"That doesn't surprise me. It's the killing. She says I ought to be ashamed of myself." His apprehension disappeared as the familiar flow of the past began to carry him along. "They don't mind you saying you were glad to win the war, but God help you if you say you were glad to kill a German."

The boy grinned, and once again the old man saw himself mirrored. "I was old to be a paratrooper, but if you were in good shape and wanted it badly enough, they wouldn't stand in your way. And I wanted it. I was tired of farming for my father, and your grandma and I weren't getting along too well, and anyway, the times had gotten into my blood. If it had been hippie time, I'd have been a hippie; but it was wartime, so I went to war.

"We shipped to England in the wintertime and trained near Scotland. Dropped onto the moors around dawn, with the frost on the heather bushes lighting the way. Getting the timing down, you know, because if you're a minute late, you're a mile from nowhere. We attacked a mock-up town and the sheep pasture behind it.

"Then they sent us south to the Channel and we sat. Nothing to do, not much news—just air raids and drills. We played poker and drank infirmary alcohol mixed with a chocolate drink that we'd stolen from the Navy, but after a while, sober or not, we didn't know what day it was. Then one night the drill turned out to be real, and we were airborne before dawn. They had us packed in rows facing the back of the plane, my platoon right next to the fuselage." He saw it ribbed and riveted like the inside of a boxcar, the skin of the plane swelling in and out in the dusky light, and heard the drone of the engines.

"The lieutenant repeated what we'd heard in the hangar: form fast, take the highway, take the town if we could, or go around it, take the hill behind the town and hold on. It was cold as a witch's tit and the air stank like a gas station and nobody said much. The kid next to me kept mumbling, *'Combien baiser, mademoiselle?'* in hillbilly French. Do you understand French?"

The boy nodded. "Were you scared?"

"I don't know. All I remember is wishing I could blast a hole in the side of the plane so we could get some air. Finally we passed over antiaircraft fire. You wouldn't believe what a relief it was to hear those guns. Hallelujah! Somebody's out there, and they're trying to kill us."

Carl burst out laughing. It surprised his grandfather that, from such a thin voice, the laughter could be so deep.

"Not long after, they lined us up and shot the doors open, and the hillbilly got sick on my boots. We just stood there looking at that door as if we expected somebody to climb through it. Some of us, they had to push, and by God, one fought back. I just kept my eyes on the helmet in front of me until I saw the wingtip in that little square of gray sky. The sergeant shouted, 'Go!' and I went.

"The air gave me a jolt, and the parachute, when it opened, gave me another. But I tell you, after the inside of that plane, the biggest shock was all that green down below. The reconnaissance photos had been black and white, you know? Which made it look like the kind of place where people got shot. But looking down, I kept thinking, there can't be a war here, it's too pretty."

The hills clothed in forest, the hedged black fields, the town with its Gothic church still untouched, the sun on the horizon shining through the morning haze like a lamp through a gauze curtain. And everywhere the sky was crisscrossed by double strands of falling soldiers. They were west of their target, at the edge of the woods. He had to pull back hard on the straps to keep the breeze from carrying him in. Even while he fought to stay clear of the trees, even after the man next to him dropped his arms and swung like a bob, he felt the beauty of the land below. An uneven line of collapsed parachutes spattered the fields. The line came closer, the ground seemed to leap, and he rolled down in a spray of mud.

"The Army doesn't teach you to think."

"Don't think—react!" the boy agreed.

"They know the man who thinks is going to end up dead, so they put a little switch into your brain—see the enemy/hit the dirt. You'll find that's a sound bit of advice. Anytime you see trouble—bill collectors, preachers, salesmen—hit the dirt!" the old man whooped. "They'll get you in the end, but by God you can take a few of them with you.

"Anyway, there I was trying to wad up the chute, the field spinning around me like a circus horse, when all of a sudden a machine-gun burst ripped through the canvas

and made a hole right through my cloud of breath. So
what did I do?"

The boy grinned. "Hit the dirt!"

"Shit, no. I ran like hell toward the woods. Didn't run
for cover, didn't look back, just ran. Even when I got to
the trees I kept going, till I got so far in I began to be more
afraid of what lay ahead than what I was running from.
So much for training. I sat on a log to catch my breath
and cleaned the mud from my rifle. It must have rained
the day before because the woods stank of wet leaves,
and there were puddles. Sitting there, I saw, for the first
time, one of those stone huts with the sod roof and a
cockeyed window near the door, and saw the gun flashes
from the window. That's the strange thing about running
scared—you don't notice much at the time, but later on,
when you stop, it comes to you.

"I turned around and went back almost to the edge of
the woods, looking for my unit. There was a strip of rough
pasture with the stone house at one end, a dirt road
nearby, and across the road were fields ankle-high in
wheat. The Germans were searching bodies—some of
them my friends. They looked like pieces of something
big that had fallen out of the sky and gone bust. But I
didn't think 'my friends' at the time. It just wasn't something you did. I worried about being cut off. While I
watched, three truckloads of German troops came tear-
ing down the road, heading east, and a soldier ran out of
the house to wave them down. I figured maybe I could get
around them through the woods—the fighting sounded
light. I thought in maybe fifteen or twenty minutes I could
work my way out. But this was no Illinois woods."

*The pines were tall and bunched together as if on pur-
pose to block out the light; where the light shone through,
there were alders, and the ground was tangled with
brush. He picked his way slowly, using his rifle like a
hand to push back the branches. Every few yards he*

would slip on a buried limb or lurch into a hole, making his stealth ridiculous. With the Germans out of sight, he began to populate his surroundings with imaginary enemies. In every thicket, rifles glinted. Shadows waited for him to come within range. And more than once he spun around quickly, only to discover that the footsteps he'd heard were the forest's pale echo of his own.

"It took me about five minutes to get lost, and only because I was walking so slow. It's amazing how you can know exactly where you're going, get there, and not know where the hell you are. So I wandered for a while until I stumbled across a path, which I followed because it was a path and I was lost. But then I started to get light-headed and had to hide myself behind a rock so I wouldn't faint in the open. God's truth, the minute my butt touched the ground I curled up and shook like a dog in a thunderstorm. I thought I was doing to die. I saw myself out in that wheat field with the rest, watching those bastards coming toward me, and there was nothing I could do. After the shaking quieted I sat up and listened —not for anything in particular. My mind was as blank as if I'd just woken up from a nap. Then I went on."

The forest of glints and shadows had disappeared. In its place the smell of pine needles, the rustling of trees beneath the distanceless crackle of rifle fire, the roughness of bark as he leaned on a hemlock, smoky-white shafts of sunlight angling through the trees to spotlight a circle of brush, a small tree.

"The path was actually a lot of paths. Every half mile or so it would fork, and hell, I didn't know one direction from another. I just followed the angle of light. Eventually it dawned on me that the angles should be pointing east and that the town was east, but my mind was on automatic. I walked maybe two miles, looking for a way out. A ridge rose up on the left and seemed to get steeper the farther I went. The mortars were pounding, but it was hard to tell whose was whose—the sound came from everywhere at once."

Though he tried to keep his eyes peeled for some flicker of gray ahead, what he saw were GIs running in a crouch from stone doorway to stone doorway through a town he'd never seen but which seemed more real to him than the woods because it was where he ought to be.

The old man paused for a moment. So much talking had brought a flush to his face. He touched his cheek and discovered his fingers were icy.

"Where was I?"

"The imaginary town was more compelling than the actual forest."

He snorted, partly because of his grandson's language and partly to hide his embarrassment—so he'd spoken those private thoughts. How much had he revealed? The boy's face was a blank.

"Interesting idea," Carl added.

"I don't need any psychoanalysis."

Carl set his bottle on the bench and curled his legs beneath him like an Indian.

"After a mile or so the path began to switchback up the ridge. Halfway up, it came to a kind of plateau with huge gray rocks scattered over it. For the first time in a long while I could see the sky—light blue and not a cloud anywhere. In the middle of the plateau was a tall pine loaded with starlings the battle had chased from the fields. I got rid of my pack and helmet and climbed a tree to have a look. But the hill on the right wouldn't give me a view of the fighting. All I could see was where I'd been, which didn't look like much—a nice, gentle slide downhill—and I thought, nobody but an idiot could get lost there.

"Then I saw little flashes of light, the kind a fish makes when he swims near the surface, and they were coming toward me. They stopped and started again, and I strad-

dled a branch and watched. I'd seen so much trouble that
wasn't there, I didn't believe my eyes. But when it started
up the third time, near the bottom of that hill, I slid down
the tree like a fireman—scraped half the skin off my
hands. The suddenness of it must have scared the birds
because that big pine exploded. You should have seen it!''

*They rose up with a single shriek, keeping the shape of
the tree in their flight. Even in their terror, they did not
break away but slued back and forth, giving the flock the
appearance of a man trying to fight his way out of a sack.
Then slowly they returned. The sunlight flickered on their
wings, and the tree became what it had been.*

*Again he ran, but this time he ran easily, the rifle
swinging from one hand, the other flung out for balance.
The enemy! The young soldier felt a strange thrill. On the
far side of the plateau, the path split, one branch climbing
farther up the ridge while the other dipped to follow a
stream.*

"I figured that sooner or later the stream had to reach
the farmland below the town, so I took the low road. It
was prettier, too. The slope was rocky, but there were
yellow flowers everywhere. The stream and the path
went down nice and easy, like a double set of stair steps,
into the forest.''

*The sun fell behind the ridge as he descended. Once
into the shade of the pines, he could see his breath again
—and the trail of the bullets. The creek bank had grown
steeper. Small trees, half-uprooted, leaned over it, and in
places the bank had cut into the path. This side of the
plateau, the rain from the night before had seeped into
the ground. In some low spots the path had disintegrated,
and dozens of boot tracks cut their own trails across the
mud.*

The old man stopped talking and tried to envision his
helmet and pack. Where were they? In forty years of
telling this story, he'd never left them behind. But his

memory was playing tricks on him. There he was, clear as day, a squat, black-haired man without a pack, pounding the butt of his rifle on a tree that had fallen near the path and cursing himself for forgetting them. It was as if the part where he'd picked up his gear again had been washed away, and the story had continued without it. Bewildered, he went on, listening now to his own words as the young soldier listened to the forest.

Because there were no shafts of sunlight, he could not tell direction, but soon the stream curved around an incline and he knew he had reached the hill that had blocked his view. A humped wooden bridge crossed the stream, but the path it led to, after skirting a couple of soggy glades, returned to parallel his own on the opposite side. Then a crease appeared in the hill. The creek veered toward it, drew in its banks, gathered speed, and plunged straight down into a narrow ravine. Leaning cautiously over a steel railing bolted to the rock shelf at his feet, he peered over the edge. The water spread like a fan as it fell and broke into spray on a heap of boulders below. But instead of gathering itself together, the water dispersed into a rocky marsh. A mist hung around the trees like smoke, and there was a sharp, ripe smell that reminded him of silage.

Running his fingers over the pitted bar, he tried to picture what this spot might mean to the people of the town. He could hear them puffing as they clambered up the trail, holding on to a rope that was threaded through metal loops embedded in the rock. He saw them leaning over to watch the falls, carrying their baskets across the humpbacked bridge to one of the glades, where German soldiers were searching the bodies of the dead. He saw the townspeople spreading their picnic cloths to the sound of mortars and rifle fire. Overhead, the flight of starlings rushed by like a black river, with a sound not very different from that of the falls.

The path at the bottom lay more or less underwater, but there were blazes on tree trunks and strips of cloth tied to bushes. No way he could tell the footing. Rocks went swimming under his weight; boggy spots turned out to be hard underneath. Several times he lurched into water above his knees. His feet went numb, and the rest of him ached. Yet he sloshed forward from blaze to blaze, happy as a hog because he was getting through. Somewhere on the other side of this foolishness, he would come out into the open: there would be a town or a highway or fields; there would be real soldiers fighting a real battle and dying real deaths.

Feeling a young man's eagerness, and knowing how it would end, the old man trembled as if he were already running along the edge of the meadow through a dapple of sunlight and shade.

Mist hung everywhere over the water, with winds too light for him to feel, hiding nothing but playing tricks on the eyes. He would halt, casting about for the next blaze, and find it on a tree he'd looked at twice before; a strip of white cloth tied to a bush would be gone when he got there or transformed into a bit of soggy gray newspaper in German. Even then, this obscuring and revealing had seemed magical, as though there were someone just ahead laying down the path and if he hurried, he might catch up.

Soon the ravine began to widen, islands of solid ground appeared, and the pine woods crept into the basin. He worried about what would happen when he returned to his own lines, to men who were not his friends and who would wonder where he had been. What could he say? That a machine gun had chased him into the forest and a couple of hours later he'd wandered out? Lost, they would say. There were plenty of ways to desert. If he could tell them, "I heard a runner coming toward me. I waited in ambush, and here is the message he carried." But he had nothing to show.

The walls of rock grew green, relaxed and sprawled into the trees, the marsh shrank to a creek, and once more he walked a path torn by bootprints. The mist still drifted above the water—thicker, it seemed, for being penned in—and the path weaved in and out of it. The ravine slipped behind a nub of the hill. The soldier glanced over his shoulder, saw nothing, and was satisfied. He listened but heard only the intermittent rifle fire and the thump of his own footsteps. Gradually it dawned on him that he was listening to an absence. The mortars had stopped.

But knowing the cause merely added to his unease. The forest had paused to wait. He could feel himself drawn forward.

In the mist ahead was a wavering shadow (he would say, "A runner broke from the mist"), as if someone had answered his fear ("and I waited for him to come within range"). The shadow resolved vaguely into the figure of a man, but the figure was not running. It appeared to be turning small circles close to the water like a man tamping down the earth around a mine. He approached slowly, ready to jump for cover, but the figure kept to its task. Something was wrong. Pinning his gun against the trunk of a tree, he shouted. No response. He shouted again. No answer. So he pulled the trigger.

"It was the first time in my life I ever shot at a man," said the old man. His grandson's chair reared onto its hind legs.

The sound of the shot echoed from the ravine, and somewhere ahead a machine gun caught the echo and sent it back. The mist leapt aside like a startled deer. He lowered his rifle and spat into the stream. "Shit."

It was one of his own—one of the bunch who played basketball on the courts next to the commissary. The dead boy circled like a pendulum in his straps, his feet just inches above the water, his parachute tangled in the trees he'd fallen through. Arms and legs bent and rigid, head lolling against the top of the pack, he looked as though he'd been frozen in midstep as he'd thrown his head back to laugh.

The old man saw himself falling, saw the spires of the cathedral, saw the swath of green below, and realized this time he would not be able to pull back. He blinked away the vision. Watching the dead man revolve to the creaking of canvas straps, he thought, I must be close to the edge of the forest. His head throbbed. All around him were dead men matting the wheat; it would be easy to lie down with them. The hand he had placed on the trunk of an alder began to shake. He snatched it away.

He'd missed, apparently. There were no wounds—he looked over the body again to make sure. Not a one. A little purple welt on the neck, and a man had become a coat hanger.

Eyeing the bindings of the dead soldier's pack, he felt a queasy "No!" in the pit of his stomach. But he needed a blanket and rations. It would be cold tonight, and God only knew whether they'd have a field kitchen. The corpse swung not far from the edge of the bank. With luck he could slip off the pack. Grabbing hold of a nearby bush, he leaned out over the water. But at the touch of that rigid arm, he flinched away, and the corpse turned in its harness as if it were trying to shrug him off. Then he caught the harness and drew the body toward him. The dead boy's head, which had been nodding in time with the revolutions, paused, then slid to the edge of the pack and stared, white-eyed, straight at him.

He let out a yelp, lost his balance, and fell backward into the stream, which dragged him a couple of yards and nearly took his feet out from under him. The water was freezing cold. As he scrambled out onto the muddy bank, a stiff foot brushed his backside. Still on his hands and knees, trembling, he let out a pure gut scream of frustration and pain that was answered somewhere in the trees above him by the shriek of a bird. Then he laughed.

The laughter caught in the old man's lungs and turned into a coughing fit that shook him from head to heel. When he'd swallowed his phlegm and begun to breathe evenly again, the man on the bank took his hands from his knees, picked up his rifle, and went on. His whole body felt numb. Out of plain stubbornness he did not look back, but he could feel the dead man's eyes burning into him like tiny disks of ice.

The path angled away from the stream, as it always had. The old man knew he would follow it till the stream was out of sight. At the top of a knoll the forest would open onto a sunlit meadow. Over a crescent of trees on his right he would see the tops of the spires. Yes, and when he walked out from the cover of the trees, the Germans would begin to shell the town from the hill above. He would be running toward the explosions, and he would not see the stranded enemy soldiers and their machine gun until he was almost on top of them. One of the soldiers, who had been lighting a cigarette, would drop it, grab his rifle by the stock and lunge wildly. The bayonet would pass under the old man's arm. He would club that man to the ground and shoot the other two before they could turn the machine gun. Then he'd swing back to the first, kneeling beside him, openmouthed and blinking, and would empty the rest of the clip into him.

The old man grunted, relieved that he could see ahead to the end. Yes, he'd been scared, he'd been lost, he had taken to shooting at shadows, but finally, almost by accident, he would kill his Germans—and from there he'd be able to find his way back.

Gun drooping, the man in the forest had continued some distance along the path, favoring his left leg despite the fact that there was no feeling in it and wearing his shame and anger as resignedly as he wore his wet and muddy clothes. The more pain he felt, the more vivid the woods around him became. The thinning stand of pines, the ground strewn with leaves, brush, fallen branches—

he saw them now as distinctly as he'd seen the flashes of gunfire from the window of the hut. Under a patch of sunlight a dark thicket spread, covered with new growth like a coat of light green fur, overrun by a tall, spiny weed with purple-rimmed leaves. In the middle of it, three small pines grew around the remains of a fallen log. Strange, he thought, and remembered the sun nosing up between the hills as he descended, checkering the town with light and shadow. He understood now that the strangeness was what made it beautiful. Because it was wrong.

As the path began to climb a shelf of white rock, he smelled nitrate. The path was sprinkled with wood chips and dirt. At the top he had to use his rifle as a cane to step around a shell crater and a small shivered birch. Trees nearby were freckled with flame-shaped wounds, each with a fragment of blackened metal burrowed into its meat. The path continued up a low knoll. Beyond its rim the outlines of the trees blurred with sunlight. He knew where he was. He walked more easily, feeling the breeze on his face, and watched the sky rise above the rim. There was a meadow glazed with white and yellow wildflowers, a macadam road, a gray frame farmhouse, and the spires of the cathedral. He approached haltingly through a dapple of sunlight and shade, and on cue, the shelling began.

Awkwardly, but without pain, he ran along the edge of the woods toward the road and across the uneven ground. The Germans behind their hillock of grass cried out. Startled, as he always was, he tried to stop, but his feet had turned to air. One of them reached for his rifle slowly and lifted his face, and the old man saw with horror that the eyes were blank. Suddenly, he felt as he had at the door of the plane, drawn forward by the rush of air outside, and he could not stop himself in time.

"No!" the old man whispered.

But the bayonet was already a cramp in his guts, and he fell to the ground. He tried to rise, but it thrust him down again. He screamed at the pain, as though his anger could hurl it back, but his head dropped onto the grass. The line of trees above him solidified into a black ring, sharp as a barrel's rim, and there were waves in the sky. Then there was no sky at all.

Where the sky had been, he heard his grandson crying, "God! Oh, God!" The old man wished he could tell him it didn't matter. The pain had disappeared, and the warmth flowing out of him gave him a fugitive pleasure. The voice that had shouted, "No!" told him he was dying, but he didn't believe it. Because the voice was too far away, and because his body was telling him it felt good.

Fiercely, then, the wounds began to hurt, and the pain brought back his sight. He lay among the white and yellow flowers staring up at the treetops, which seemed to be on fire. The soldiers were arguing in accents he remembered from his childhood, pointing to him and to the town. One was wiping his bayonet with a fistful of grass. An enemy officer stepped out from the trees and snapped an order. The soldiers, muttering to themselves, quickly broke down the gun and hurried away in the direction he had come.

The officer descended to where he lay. He was a thin young man whose yellow hair stuck out at odd angles where his helmet had been. One of his hands swung uselessly at his side, a large hand with long fingers. He knelt to look at the wound.

"*Nutzlos, mein Bekannter,*" he said, slipping a sharp-nosed pistol from his holster.

The old man tried to struggle, but he could not even lift his head. "No!" he whispered.

The young officer's grimed face cracked into a weary half smile, and he responded in English. "Haven't you killed enough of us?"

The old man looked away and contemplated the fire in the trees. The rippled sky glittered like glass, and he couldn't breathe for the thickness in his mouth. It was wrong, but that did not matter. Once again he was falling through the freezing dawn air—the hedged fields below, to the east the rolling forest and the cathedral town—and the earth was rising up to meet him.

Balance at Zero

B E F O R E she left, she said to me, "You could have been somebody."

I said, "Who?"

"You could have been a man."

I said, "I am."

Somebody. What's somebody? It's the one you've got a handle on, right? All she's saying is, she's got no handle. People don't like that. They can't hold on, so they pretend you're not there.

That's the cost of being my own man. Nobody tells me where to go or what to do when I get there, but nobody cuts me any breaks, either. Everybody wants to tie you down. You've got to fight that, and when it's no good fighting, you have to know where to find the back door. Which means traveling light. A paycheck today, a little country pie between the sheets tonight, and someplace to hunt tomorrow—that's all a man needs. The rest ain't worth the price of admission.

So I'll never make it to the top of the heap. So what? The way I figure it, you eat shit at the top and you eat shit at the bottom. At the top, it just costs you more. All I want is what's right here, right now, feels good, and doesn't ask for contributions. Don't tell me, yesterday I said this or yesterday I did that. Yesterday's another universe. You want to talk about yesterday? Find the man that was here yesterday. Sure as hell, it wasn't me.

Sandy was worse than most of them. She'd offer you so many handles, you'd go crazy figuring which one to use. Dreams, all the time dreams. And from the dreams she'd start to plan, and from the plans she'd come to expect things. Pretty soon she didn't know piss from pumpernickel.

I told her, "You don't listen to me, every con man in town's going to sell you his acre of swamp."

She said, "I've already got my acre of swamp," smiling
at me like I should catch her drift.

I ignored her. You catch people's drift, they always expect you to do something with it. It's just another way of
holding on.

She had this notebook where she used to write down
her dreams and what she thought they meant and quotes
she got out of women's magazines. You know, one of
those kiddie jobs with the wire binding and a picture of a
girl talking to a rabbit with a tux on. Once she found out
I knew about it, she locked it in a drawer like it was
money.

"I never dream," I told her.

She said, "You still dream, you just don't remember."

I said, "If I don't remember, it didn't happen."

There was one time I walked in while she had the notebook out, and I asked her what she was writing.

She closed it and hooked the pen inside the rings. "Us."

"No such animal as 'us.' If there was, I'd shoot it."

"I wouldn't be surprised. Listen, if I ask you a straight
question, will you give me a straight answer?"

"Sure."

"What do you want out of me?"

"Nothing."

You would've thought I was talking Chinese.

"Impossible. It's like dreaming, you can't help yourself."

I reminded her, "No expectations."

She tossed the notebook into the drawer. "But 'no expectations' is an expectation."

Her favorite game—twisting words around. I didn't
mind. It was just air.

. . .

But when she started hanging out with the moron, she changed. Big-time conversion. No more jokes, no more head games. I mean, everything was suddenly serious because she felt sorry for him. And once she felt sorry, she started to listen, and once she listened, she had to make it mean something.

I said, "He's retarded."

She said, "Not retarded, simple."

I told her, "You can't feel sorry for people—that's just another handle. And everybody who's got a handle is going to use it."

All this happened while I was working at a place called Xerographic Inc. in upstate New York. I fell into the job the way I've managed most of my life, following the current and looking for easy water. Back in the seventies my father tried to send me to college, and I actually spent a few weeks there, on this funny farm in Iowa for dumb rich kids, before I decided I knew better ways to waste time. So I took what was left of the money he gave me and some on loan from the government, and headed for Idaho with a couple of rifles and a case of tequila, and never looked back.

The hunting was good, but the money didn't last. It was deal drugs or burn hamburgers, and since I don't speak Spanish, I didn't feel qualified for either. I went out, got pissed, and stayed pissed till I didn't care anymore, then signed up with the Army. By the time I sobered up, I was on a bus to basic with an Idaho farm boy in the seat beside me talking about freezing bull sperm.

At first, I thought I'd really screwed my ass to the wall. But I'm not the kind that gets pushed out of shape by uniforms and regulations, so once I'd waded through basic, the Army grew on me. Sure, they've got their games, but it all comes down to: Do what you're told and say what they want to hear. They don't want *you*, they want a soldier. You give them a soldier, they'll leave you alone.

They had this idea, at first, of training me to repair planes or helicopters or something, but I didn't have the patience. So they made me what they called a "maintenance technician," which meant I repaired the machines they could afford to lose, and sent me to this warehouse complex in Texas where the Army keeps parts for everything that runs, except officers. The work was nothing—mostly maintenance on conveyors and packagers—and it felt good. I mean, once you've got the electronics down you're like God. You come in, take the shield off the controls, fiddle with the windings, and a big hunk of scrap metal becomes a conveyor. Yank a wire and it's scrap again.

I kept pretty much to myself, and the Army wives. If it hadn't been for a run-in with some bad acid, I might still be marching.

But even that didn't turn out so bad. I discovered that being honorable or dishonorable didn't matter to a company that was hard up for people to fix their machines. As long as you know an induction motor from a barbell, you can walk in wearing horns and a tail and they'll hire you. You can make more money than the foreman, and the foreman's the only one who can give you shit. If you get bored or the people wear on you, you can tell them to kiss your ass and go hunting. It's not freedom, but it ain't bad for the money.

Hunting is what keeps me sane. Me and my gun deep in the woods—nobody watching, nobody breathing my air or crowding my space—where everything I see is mine; stalking an old buck through the brush till the trees stand aside and he settles under the cross hairs. If the shot's true and he drops like a rock, there's a chill that goes right through you. It's like climbing out of a lake into the morning air. I feel clean.

When I hunt deer (and I hunt whenever I want to), all I take is the antlers. Some men, they drag out the whole fucking carcass—for meat, they say. Bullshit. If they wanted meat, they'd buy it. The shiver is what they want, but they can't tell the wife and kiddies that, so they make it sound like a trip to Safeway. Not me. I'm in it for the antlers. I don't need an alibi.

After I make my kill, I camp out. Pitch my tent near a riverbank and let my mind loose, let it grow till the sounds of the forest and the river are like voices inside me, and I'm the only man on earth. Every rock, every leaf, even the sunlight is mine. I should've been born a couple of hundred years ago when the West was just trees and Indians and people like me wandering where the mood took them. There's not enough space anymore. That's why, when I come out of the woods, the real world doesn't look so real.

Walking into Xerographic Products after three months in the Adirondacks was like Saturday morning cartoons on TV. The door went *whoosh* before I could touch the handle, and there was a receptionist with earphones on like a pilot. I filled the application with so many lies, I had to keep looking back a page to remind myself who I was. The interviewer duck-walked over to me, offered his hand, and gave mine one quick jerk as if I was a slot machine. He asked the usual questions, and I told more lies. He didn't believe them, but as long as the story held together, it was no skin off his back. He hired me for the swing shift and congratulated me on my "impressive résumé." On the way out, I damn near steered my truck into the gate, I was laughing so hard.

Guys like him don't bother me, though. He's a phony, but he knows it, and he knows the whole setup is phony, too, so he just plays along. The other type, the ones who are in it for real, they're the scary ones.

. . .

The first days were the worst. Every morning was like waking up with a hangover. There had been rain most of that week, a cold rain, and the basement of the place I'd rented was flooded. A mildewed smell came up through the floorboards and stank up the whole house. Since the company hadn't given me my ID yet, I had to wait at the gatehouse for someone to come for me. The shift filed through—men with that squared-off look you get when you lift things a lot—not talking much, slipping their ID cards into a slot and waiting for the snap that unlocked the turnstile. In the shadow of the gatehouse I could see their breath gather into a cloud and fade over the fence like the smoke from my cigarette. It depressed me. I wanted to bust my way through, but I just leaned against the gatehouse, lighting matches and tossing them into a trash barrel. When I looked up, this bulldoggy man was staring at me from the other side of the gate.

I knew the first time we met, he hated my guts. His name was Ben Woodall, and he was the foreman. That's all he said till we got inside. I wondered how old he was. His hair had gone white, and he had a neck like the head of a pencil somebody'd whittled down.

He was all business. "Warehouse," he said. "Coating materials on this side. Through the doors you've got storage for the Converting and Shipping departments." He pointed to a couple of overhead doors in the far wall.

Around us on wooden skids were big rolls of white paper, lined up on either side of two dirty aisles in half-assed rows like a regiment of spastics. A man went by pulling a hand truck with a yellow barrel on it. A white breathing mask dangled around his Adam's apple; a skull and crossbones was stenciled on the side of the barrel.

"Poisonous?" I asked.

"And explosive."

He nodded toward an opening about the size of two garage doors where the man with the truck was headed.

Through it I could see a forklift slide one of those rolls onto a machine.

"Coating. That's where the paper is treated and wrapped, then it's stored in the warehouse next door until Converting cuts it to order." He waved toward the machine. "Those old monsters, you don't need to worry about them—they're under a service contract. You'll spend your time—most of it anyway—on the cutting floor."

His office was a glass-and-wallboard hut in a corner of the warehouse that he shared with a file clerk and a couple of label printers. It was packed with men from the day shift adding up their work logs and smelled of Goop and perfume. While the men pushed through to drop their sheets into a wire basket on his desk, he ran me through a sieve. How much did I know about this or that machine? Where did I learn it? How long did I do it? My answers seemed to satisfy him, but he kept squinting at the thumb he was running along the edge of his desk.

After a while he loosened up, and we traded hunting stories. He was one of those cut-'em-up-in-the-garage types. A few men from the swing shift came by to shake my hand and joke about the guy I was replacing, who'd cracked his head falling off a roll he'd tried to use as a ladder. I told them about my last day in the woods shooting beer cans off a stump with my .22, and how I'd got a kind of balance going—the more I drank, the worse my aim; the better my aim, the more I needed cans. It cracked them up.

Woodall scratched his ear and said, "Here's your man, Bud. He's a marksman."

A guy behind me stuck out a spongy little hand. "Hey, how about that? I raise dogs."

I should have quit right then.

He was Woodall's height, but built the way kids draw a man: big round body, round head, with tubes for arms and legs. His eyes were as wide as a doll's, and he was bald and slow and fussy. He carried around a hand-carved pipe with a lid on it that he was always fiddling with or leaving behind. He was what you might call a nice man. Five minutes with him and you wanted a bale of whatever he put in that pipe; ten, and you wanted to add arsenic. It was like being handed a baby.

After the day shift cleared, Bud took me through the Converting section of the warehouse. Behind a group of tall, uneasy stacks of skids and box material were the same batallions of paper rolls, covered in black plastic. The stacks worried me. I could see some jeep jockey cutting around the corner with his forks up and turning me into a shish kebab. Sandy called me para-noid, but I tell you, I'd sooner take on a carload of cops with an empty gun than walk up to a corner I can't see around.

We took our time because Bud had to stop every ten feet or so to relight his pipe and tell me about his daugh-ter the lawyer or his other daughter who ran track in high school and his dogs and his house and his truck and his wife.

"The younger one can run three miles under fifteen minutes. The lawyer can't go to the store without a car. . . . Here we make twenty different types of photosensi-tive paper—blueprint paper, engineering paper, film for advertising graphics. . . . Don't take me wrong, she's a good kid. Represents an ad agency in Chicago, makes a lot of money. She has one of those toy collies, pitiful-looking thing. . . . Pull the red cord if you want to open the door, the black cord if you want to close it. . . . I raise retrievers, myself. What sort of hunting do you do?"

"Any kind I want," I said, and pulled the red cord.

While Bud lagged to get the last out of his pipe, I stepped through onto the cutting floor. There was an in-credible rush of noise. The floor throbbed, and clouds of

dust eddied around deep yellow lights (yellow to protect
the paper), and a dark, churning mass of machinery
heaved in the Halloween glow.

Bud came up behind me. "Welcome to the family!" he
shouted.

I damn near jumped out of my shoes.

Take maybe fifty machines, and if you're new to the
work, you'd think it'd take a fucking genius to get them
all down. But it's no big deal once you sort them out.
Every machine but one ran off an induction motor—the
conveyors used capacitors, the sheeters and roll cutters
worked by repulsion. Only the cutting mechanisms were
new to me. Bud ushered me from one to another and
gossiped with the operators about his dogs and his daughters. Most of it got lost in the noise.

The cutters were lined up in hollow squares facing narrow aisles, where the handlers on small three-wheeled
forks called tow motors loaded and unloaded them.
Aisles so narrow, when a tow motor passed we had to
stand aside, with some damned cutter whirring and chop-
ping at our asses. And they'd jammed the machines together as tight as they could, with only one opening on
each side, like the alley in the middle of a city block, that
let out onto the aisles.

The buzzer sounded for break, and one by one the machines shut down like lights going out in a skyscraper. On
the way to the lounge, we passed a door with a red cau-
tion sign blinking above it. I asked what was inside.

"X-ray film coaters. The company's trying to diversify."
Bud shook his head. "I wouldn't want to work in there."

"Why not?"

"You can't see what you're doing." He stopped, suddenly, and slapped the flat of his hand with his fist.
"Damn! I was going to show you 'O.' Remind me, and
we'll go after break."

I said, "Yeah," but I didn't bother, and he forgot.

. . .

What I remember of the next few weeks, other than ro-
tors and blades, is mostly Bud tamping his pipe with a
bolt off one of the packagers. Sometimes I wanted to stuff
him into that fancy carved bowl and light a match. Hell,
cripples on crutches moved faster. When he worked, it
was like he was underwater. He had this philosophical
thing about a machine. He couldn't just fix it, he had to
worry about how it got that way. Talk to it, sniff it, try all
the wires. A job I'd be in and out of in fifteen minutes
took Bud an hour.

Me, I can't go that slow, I'd explode. A stack of job
sheets is a weight, and the sooner I get it off my back, the
better. Then I've earned my keep, and I can do what I
want. If the foreman comes looking for me, I've got the
best disappearing act in town. Everybody's just seen me,
but nobody knows where I am. Maybe that won't win
awards, but the job gets done, and I don't have to baby-
talk gear assemblies to do it. I don't grudge a man his
style, but when you're the slow car on the road, you learn
to get out of the way. Unless, like Bud, you think that line
makes you the leader.

He was all the time crowding me. It wasn't enough for
me to stick a bearing into a conveyor, I had to go through
this bullshit routine like it was Air Force One or something. For instance, every cutter has a safety pedal—
the blades won't drop if the pedal's not down, so when the
pedal on one of the roll cutters shorted and froze the
machine, I found a wire that had been rubbed bare and
taped it.

You'd have thought I had wrapped it in tinfoil. "No,
no!" he shouted. "You need to replace that wire and
check the system to be sure there aren't more like it."

I figured he was giving advice. I mean, the cutter
worked. What more did he want? But when I went to

screw on the plate, he grabbed my arm and cried, "Damn it, no!" His round face bunched up like a fist.

I had to waste half an hour finding out what I already knew: there was nothing else wrong with the cutter.

At the end Bud was all smiles. "See? Isn't that better?"

"Sure." I stepped on the pedal, and the blade smacked down, almost in the old bastard's lap. He jumped about ten feet in the air, and his mouth opened so wide you could have driven a train through it.

"Much better," I said.

I never did find a way around him, though. Once I knew the machines, we split a lot of the jobs. There were days I was all to myself. Still, I'd have to look over my shoulder to make sure Mr. Right wasn't sneaking up behind me. Now and then, I'd catch Woodall watching me from the aisle, his lips puckered up.

In the lunchroom it didn't matter where I sat, Bud would float down nearby like a big balloon and start in on the dogs and daughters. Or on me.

Which he did more and more often as time went on, lighting up his pipe and asking me, offhand, where I came from, what my parents did, if I'd played any sports in school. I'd answer whatever came into my head: my parents died in a fire, my sister married an Arab when she was fourteen, I'd worked for Army intelligence. Any crazy thing. He'd sit back with his head sunk in his chins trying to piece me together. But the game started to piss me off after a while. Him, it never seemed to faze. Those wide baby eyes would steady on me as though my head was a stator full of wires and he was looking for the ones that had crossed. He'd let out a cloud of smoke that would rise up and float away, and his eyes wouldn't move, even when he was laughing. They were softer than Woodall's but there was something scary in the softness—like if I hit him, I might not get my hand back.

Some days, after I left the factory, I felt trapped. Too

many cars on the road, too many windows with lights in them. I'd drive by the run-down farmhouse I rented, sure that somebody had broken a window and was waiting inside. Instead of going home, I'd haunt the country roads —with my lights off, sometimes, for the strangeness of it —till I felt like myself again.

The next afternoon I'd walk into Converting. There'd be the same rush of noise and the yellow light that would melt through my skin. Woodall would just be Woodall and Bud would be Bud and the job was only a job. But I'd still find myself wishing I could say, "Yes, sir," and salute.

Somewhere along the line, Bud remembered "O." It was one of his down days—I could tell because he always got philosophical when he felt bad. At the break he stared at his coffee as if it had gone solid on him. The packager beside him asked what was wrong, and he shrugged. Come to find out later, daughter number one was sleeping with a married man.

Right before we went back to work, out of the blue he said to the packager, "We're odd creatures, aren't we, Jerry? We go through life saying, 'I don't know everything, but at least I know this—this little corner of the puzzle,' until the truth gives us a kick in the pants. So we narrow the claim, as much as to say, 'If I make the pieces small enough, I'll be fine,' which gets us another kick in the pants. It makes you wonder."

All that because some married man was humping his daughter.

Jerry was used to it. He went on munching his fried pie and said, "I suppose," raining blueberry spit all over the table.

After lunch Bud told me to come with him, and we headed into Coating. I expected something along the lines of the cutting floor, but it was like walking into a time machine. Coaters as big as dinosaurs, but so quiet you could hear your own footsteps. There were yards of space between them. An acid stink in the air. It felt like walking through a tall forest, where there's no brush and no smell but pine.

The machines had letter names. Bud gave me a sermon on "C," which they didn't use anymore—a huge, long, complicated sucker—jabbing at it with his pipe stem to make his points.

"This is the old way: see how complex the gearing is, how it shifts direction here and here and again over here? So many parts to go wrong, and the slow speed tends to wrinkle the paper. The inventor saw four jobs and created four machines in one. No imagination."

Then he grabbed my hand as if I was a kid. I snatched it back. I hate men who put their hands on you.

We followed a nigger with a mask on pulling one of those yellow barrels with the skull and crossbones on the side into a hangar-size area, a couple of stories higher than the rest of the factory. There stood a machine that took up as much space as your average grade school and was shaped like one of those laughing Buddhas that soldiers bring home from the East: clean roll and bath at one knee, coated roll at the other, and a pyramid frame of stainless-steel rollers in between. Another nigger leaned over a console at its feet. The paper went up one side and down the other—that was it.

I watched Bud. His eyes were as wide as a baby's. "This is 'O,' " he said.

My eyes followed the man with a barrel of chemicals. I thought, I'm breathing that shit.

"One-twentieth the number of moving parts. No compressors. No fans. Four processes in one movement, so fast and so perfectly controlled, the speed itself dries the paper."

I didn't answer. What could I say? The paper went up, it came down.

"This is the kind of imagination that creates the future!"

I couldn't help myself. There he was, red as a boy in a

whorehouse, breathless over a hunk of steel. I laughed.
His face bunched up the way it did when I taped the wire,
but this time he turned on his heel and huffed off without
me, which made me laugh even harder.

About that time I was cruising the bars pretty heavy, from
boredom mostly. One of them was called Patches. Instead
of wallpaper, it had these scraps of cloth in all different
colors and shapes covering the walls. I used to go there a
lot because whatever you looked like, whoever you were,
you fit. You didn't have to put out a lot to meet women. If
you sat at the bar long enough, they'd come to you. That's
where I met Sandy.

I'd seen her at Xerographic. She ran a label printer on
the day shift. When I came to work, I knew right away
where she was by the pack of ten or twelve men with
their hands in their pockets, standing off to one side. It's
the same in a factory as it is in the Army. Any halfway hot
number can play mama-dream fuck for the whole outfit.
Sandy was the type: unnatural blonde with a decent body
and a could-have-been-pretty face that looked as though
it had gone a couple of rounds with a blackjack. I like
them tough. Tough women are good for what ails you. But
I don't stand in line, so I left her to them.

One night I walked into Patches, and before I'd got ten
feet I knew she was there, too. She wore only one kind
of perfume and wore enough of it to strangle an ox. At
the factory you would see men stop in their tracks and
stare off into space, and you'd know they had crossed her
path.

She was sitting at a table near the bar, wearing one of
those sweaters with the holes in them and a black bra
underneath, holding hands with some muscle-bound kid
who looked about nineteen.

I fed the games a couple of quarters and watched a

three-piece suit get hustled out of a twenty by the house pool shark, while the local yokels glared at the Yankees on big-screen TV.

I hate sports. I hate watching, and I hate being watched, and the rules are all wrong—they won't let you disappear.

When I went back for a refill, Sandy was leaning her cunt against an unplugged jukebox they use for decoration, pushing buttons as if she expected something to happen. Head in his hands, elbows propped on the table, young Muscles was talking to a wet bar napkin. She'd drunk him into the ground. I laid my hand on her shoulder, and she took her sweet time turning around.

I said, "What's your pleasure?"

She said, "Gin." Not even looking at me, like I was the bartender.

"Gin and what?"

"Ice."

I thought: This is my kind of woman.

With the drinks I got darts, and we played 301, loser buys the round. She was good. Aimed too much, but there was a lot of gin between her and the board. We talked a little, but mostly we played. Every time I put a hand on her she'd push it off, but she didn't say stop.

Finally, I got tired of the act. I said, "How about we put something real on the line. You win, I take a hike."

She smiled. "I like that. What happens if I lose?"

I made a little tunnel with one hand and ran a finger in and out, and stepped aside so she couldn't knee me. She held my eyes, thinking it over, then reached around and stabbed me in the ass with a dart. Hurt like hell.

"Fuck yourself," she said, the same way she'd said, "Gin." The smile was still on her face.

I didn't expect her to stick around, but I put the game on the board anyway, and she doubled in. Meanwhile, on the yokel side, the Yankees won, and some really wrecked fat bitch started dancing on the bar, grinding her lard ass and shaking her jugs. It made me want to retch. The baseball people were cheering and egging her on.

Sandy was down to forty before I doubled in, but she missed doubling out and got stuck at two. I got a lock on the twenty and worked my way down, but she couldn't hit the double-one to save her soul. We passed the darts back and forth, and I marked my scores on the board. The closer I got, the wilder her throws became.

Some skinny faggot with a beard climbed onto the bar and was bumping and grinding, too. The crowd was screaming as if somebody had opened up the doors and let the river in.

First try, I doubled out—twenty, twenty, double-ten. Sandy took the darts from me as I was wiping off the board. Now that it didn't matter, she doubled out and afterward threw a couple that didn't even hit the cork.

She stood on her toes and leaned on me like she wanted to kiss me. "Men are shits," she said.

I laughed.

"Shits," she repeated. But when I went for my coat, she put hers on, too.

As we left, the fat girl and the faggot were sitting on the edge of the bar, stretching back and mouthing like fish while the bartender poured a bottle of champagne over their heads.

Every night with Sandy was like that night all over again. The routine never changed—the ice, the games, the bullshitting, the giving in. She hated me. I think she even hated fucking me, but she liked giving in. You could see it in her face. She always fucked with her eyes closed, as if she was asleep and what her body did was happening in some dream.

But, hey, what do I care? Sex is sex any way you get it,

and with Sandy, you got it straight—none of that kissy-face or lickety-split stuff, just down and dirty, and as much as you wanted. We got along because I've got a prick like a rock—that's what she liked. None of this one-shot, hair-trigger business. I could cuss her, I could tell her what an ugly bitch she was, I could pinch her so hard she'd cry, none of it mattered to her. She just kept her eyes closed and bit down hard on her lower lip, the way she did when something scary was happening on TV.

The dream fuckers said I ruined her, meaning I ruined her for them. No more perfume, no more see-through sweaters, no more wet dreams. I like my women mine, and I like other people to know it.

As long as it was just sex and I didn't leave any scars, that was fine with her. Most women, once it gets to be a regular thing, either they're playing you off against Joe Blow or they're trying to sew you into the sheets. With Sandy, I could come and go as I pleased, if I didn't do either one too often. The whole time I knew her, she came out to my place maybe twice, and all she ever said about it was that I ought to clean out the basement. "Committed non-commitment" was what she called it.

I didn't give a damn what she called it as long as she was there when I walked in the door and I didn't have to wait in line.

Now and then, she'd try to figure me out. I'd tell her, "Curiosity's a disease," but that didn't wash, and in the end I'd have to tell her lies. When she got tired of the lies, she'd start to play shrink. "What comes to mind when I say . . . ?" But I wouldn't play. I had enough of that when I was a kid.

It's all war games anyway, seeing how much territory you can steal before the other one fights back.

· · ·

When Bud found out what was happening between me and Sandy, he didn't talk so much—just looked real sad and complained about the heat. But good things never last. Pretty soon, he hauled me into Coating, and we sat on "C" while he told me the Story.

I don't remember the details because it pissed me off having to listen. It wasn't my fault, what happened to her six or seven years ago. What it came down to, without all the soap opera, was a smart, pretty girl married a smart, pretty guy, and things didn't end up so smart and pretty. Big deal.

Smart guy had these fits of temper at work. People at work got pissed, so he decided to have them at home instead. The doctors gave them long names, which made everybody feel better. He felt so good, he pushed the pretty girl down a flight of stairs.

She left him. Friends tried to help them get back to-gether. He took little blue pills twice a day. He got a new job, they bought a house, she got pregnant, and one day he rearranged her ribs with a hammer. Exit man to prison and the baby to wherever.

There was a long pause, in case I wanted to break into tears or something.

"He was only in jail for three years. When he got out, he tried to contact her, but she wouldn't see him, so he killed himself. I don't think she'll ever forgive him for killing the baby or herself for what happened to him."

There was another long pause. He'd handed me the past like a down machine, as if he expected me to fix it.

"That's why she's so cynical," he added.

"She's not cynical," I said. "She's having a good time."

Bud relit his pipe for about the hundredth time. "In a way you've got a point. She's terribly sentimental. I sup-pose, when the mind pretends to be strong, the heart can do what it wishes. You need to help her bring the two together."

"I don't fuck with other people's problems."

His face tightened up. I'd wrapped another wire wrong.

"Don't become one of hers," he said, and I got the feeling it wasn't advice.

A couple of days later, I got another version of the Story from the girl who ran the label printer on swing shift. Then people who'd never talked to me before had something to say. I couldn't shit without some guy in the next stall giving me advice. The only person I didn't hear it from was Sandy. The whole time I knew her, she only mentioned that husband once, and it had to do with the garden in her backyard. He'd planted something or wanted something planted—I don't remember.

Every one of them ended up looking at me the same way Bud had. Their eyes followed me. The factory became one of those crazy houses lined with mirrors. Every time I looked around I'd see myself a different shape.

The voice in my gut said, "Take a hike." And I should've listened. But I'd bought a new truck and some new guns, and nothing had changed with Sandy.

Once I threatened to leave, but she just shrugged, said, "Fine," and meant it. Maybe that's why I stayed.

It was almost winter, but I started going outside on breaks anyway to shake off the eyes. I'd wander along the cyclone fence where I could see the river and the factories on the other side burning with light.

One day it rained. I was sitting on the bench in the washroom having a smoke, and Bud floated down across from me, the butts pail between us.

He said, "What's wrong?"

I took a drag and ran the toe of my shoe through a puddle of muddy water the men had brought in on their boots.

He lit his pipe. "I don't want to interfere, I want to help."

"I don't need help, I need space."

He let out a big cloud of smoke and shook his head. "It must be difficult, always on guard. Wouldn't it help if you told someone what you're fighting? Who knows? Maybe we could fight it together."

I took a drag and threw my cigarette into the pail. A crowd was pressing in on me.

"People give up hope too easily. Nothing's ever really broken," he said, pointing at me with the stem of that goddamned pipe.

I yanked it away from him and waited till he realized what I was up to and knew he couldn't stop me, then I smashed it on the floor.

"Fix that!" I shouted.

On the cutting floor the noise of the machines washed over me, and I breathed it.

Nothing changed. Bud stayed clear, but he still smiled at me when we passed and complained about the weather while we waited for Woodall to hand out the job sheets. I thought, You spineless son of a bitch.

It seemed that every day when I'd come to work there'd be the two of them, Bud and Sandy, over in a corner. He would be talking and she'd be sitting on her hands, looking down at the gap between her legs as if she wished it would go away. It got so bad that when she talked to me, I could hear him whispering underneath. In bed, she'd stare up at me while we fucked, like there was a tangle of wires below my Adam's apple that she was trying to sort out. Sometimes it spooked me. I'd stay hard, but I couldn't come. Once, I got so mad, I damn near strangled her—probably would have, except I came first.

Another night, she locked herself in the bathroom while I took a crowbar to the drawer where she kept her notebook, but it was empty.

So when the dog came, it wasn't just a dog. It was

everything. I drove over and found the porch covered
with newspapers and a golden retriever pup yowling at
the door, shit all over.

Sandy said, "Look what Bud gave me."

And the dog came splashing through its own piss and
tried to climb my leg. That was all I needed. I got a garbage bag and drove to the nearest bridge and threw the
fucking dog in the river.

I didn't have a brick. If I'd had a brick, the bag would
have sunk, and I could've gone home happy. But it didn't
sink. It surfaced and rolled along a crease in the water till
it lodged against a bar. I'm not crazy. I knew it was a bag,
I knew there was a dog in it, but that's not how it felt. It
felt like one of those nightmares you have when you're a
kid: something washed up from the river bottom that
wanted me, climbing that silt bar and slipping back,
climbing and slipping back, its black skin shining. Finally
it gave a kind of jump, fell into the current, and went
under, and I could breathe again.

From there, I drove like a bat out of hell miles before a
cop pulled me over. I went home, drank some beers, tried
to sleep, but what I kept seeing was that bag struggling
toward me out of a dark crease in the water. The next
day, I had to call in sick.

That ended it with Sandy. She changed the locks. About
a week later, Woodall took me aside, massaging that
whittled neck with his hand.

"The company is adding a maintenance man to the
night shift. Take it."

I said, "I don't want it."

He said, "Take it anyway."

"This is a union shop. You can't touch me."

The old man said, "Want to bet?" and glowed as if I'd
handed him a boxful of money.

. . .

When you move to nights, it's not just shifts you're changing, it's planets. Like living in a town of left-handers,
everything's ass backwards. You open the bars and close
the diners. People are partying at two in your afternoon,
and in the middle of your night, the city decides to put in
a water main the next street over. You go out at break
and there's a boy dressed like a girl leaning on the window of a Mercedes parked in front of the video store.

The first night, I felt this incredible high. The woman
was history, Bud was history. It was just me and the
place. Since no shipments went out at night, there was no
guard at the gate. The asphalt yard was deserted. As I
crossed it, my shadow stretched all the way to the door.
My old shift checked me out, but nobody said anything.
We were going in opposite directions.

The night foreman came in late, and Woodall had to
help him find the forms. He wheezed when he brushed
the snow off his jacket, wheezed when he shook my hand.
"Ferris," he said. "Warren Ferris." Once he'd settled
into his chair, he began to scratch his nose, which was
purple and shapeless.

He leaned a pair of wire-rimmed glasses against his
nose and studied my file. "So you're the fellow who
drowned Bud Moore's dog," he chuckled, squinting as
though he was reading it out of the folder. He blinked up
at me. "Don't worry, I ain't gonna give you no dog."

I waited for him to get around to business, but he
didn't. He kept wanting to know about the dog. Finally, I
asked, "Have you got some special way you want the
work done?"

He hefted himself forward to where he could prop his
elbows on the desk. "No. Whatever works is fine. This is
a skeleton shift, you'll be on your own."

He pushed his lunch pail aside and pointed to the bottom slot of the desk file. "The job orders will be in here.
Take a day's worth, do the jobs, fill out a plausible time

sheet—that's all I ask." When he finished, he was panting like a bicycle pump.

I said, "We're going to get along."

Which irritated him somehow. "They send me all the shits," he groused. "I had a hundred men on this shift. And more work than they could handle. Now we're down to twenty, and if management had any guts, we'd all be gone." He pinched his nose and grinned at the handle of his lunchpail. "So don't strain yourself. You might remind them we exist."

Nothing on the cutting floor was the same. With only ten or twelve machines going at a time, you didn't get that big rush of sound—only this one and that, and the dust around them like a halo. I could walk the aisles and not be afraid of what might be coming up behind me.

After the shifts changed, Ferris would disappear. They said he carried a virgin fifth of Canadian Mist in that lunchpail and spent his nights in the storage room sleeping. Maybe he did, maybe he didn't. I never bothered to find out. For a while, out of habit, I'd glance over my shoulder to see who was watching. It felt weird not to see anybody.

Since most of the machines were shut down, the jobs were mostly maintenance. The first couple of weeks, I busted ass to finish them, then I headed out to the warehouse and made myself a nest between the rolls. It was hard to get used to a space around me that wasn't mine or anybody else's, that was just things that weren't happening.

Later, to keep from boring myself to death, I'd play around with the work. I'd fool with the controls till the feed-and-cut was running backward or I'd bypass the pedal and sit back and watch the thing chop away with nothing coming out. (In the Army I once saw a guy go through a whole rifle routine—present arms, shoulder arms—with nothing in his hands. It seemed like a joke at first, but when you got into the rhythm, it began to look more real than the real thing.) The other men got into it, too. Sometimes they'd shut down to watch what I was doing—except for Frank, who couldn't figure out what was going on, and a man named Winslow Taylor, who didn't want to. Most of them had my sense of humor. Tell them you drove down country roads with your lights off, and they'd ask if you'd run over any dogs. I can't say that I liked them, but we got along. I stayed out of their way, and they stayed out of mine.

There was a red-haired packager and a couple of materials handlers who would sometimes rally tow motors for bets. There was a kid who popped reds and a man with tattoos all over him, who took his shirt off when he worked. There were niggers running "O," and there was Taylor, who got the shakes if he didn't put out more than thirty thousand yards a night. Then there was Frank.

Two Franks, really. Below the neck, he was a pint-size Arnold Schwarzenegger, with hands so big, one of them could lift a man by his skull or crush it like an egg. Above, he was wide at the jaw, his head sloping up to a peak like the sides of a tent. He was as light as I am, but he had the nose and lips and the fringe of kinky hair around his bald head that told you he had dark blood.

Frank was a moron—a real one, I read his file. The company got some kind of break from the government for hiring him. Every day he came to work in black pants and a T-shirt so white you wanted to wipe your hands on it. He knew everybody's name, and everybody was "mister," and whatever you told him he believed.

He wasn't a total retard. He could read and write and count, up to a point. But he couldn't connect. At lunch, he'd walk around with a newspaper in his hand asking questions. Why did the president say this? Why did the terrorists do that? He was sure one of us could tell him.

At break, he'd sit alone or sometimes Taylor and the pill popper would sit with him. Most of us crowded around a long table next to the vending machines. The niggers either sat off by themselves or sat in a group at the long table, but they wouldn't get anywhere near Frank. If you wanted to get a rise out of them, all you had to do was hint he was one of them.

Occasionally, for the fun of it, we'd ride him. Someone would say, "Frankie, I hear Ferris caught you pissing in the 'G' bath."

Then he'd whine in that little-girl voice he had, "I did not! I'm not that bad. You know I'm not."

When he heard the laughs, his head would slue as if he'd been kicked, and he'd go, "Ha! Ha! Ha!"

Maybe he knew he was being had, but he could never tell when. I'd say, "It's cold outside," and he'd laugh like nobody could put that over on him. Later, I'd tell him a plane had landed in the yard, and he'd run out to take a look.

Sometimes he'd stare out the window at the rain melting the snow, and it would make him cry because his brother was run over by a car—that's what he said. I found out later that it happened when Frank was ten, but with Frank, ten years or ten minutes was pretty much the same. Even the tears were funny, like watching a mountain cry.

What surprised me was the time Sandy spent with him. During switch-over to the day shift, if she wasn't fenced in by the boys with their hands in their pockets, she was off to the side with King Kong. She'd hold his hand, pat him on the knee; once I saw her kiss him. From what people said, that had been going on even when I had been seeing her, and I never knew a thing about it. I didn't go near her when she was with Frank. It would have been too easy for her to sic him on me.

One morning I asked her what she thought she was doing.

She shoved her hands in her pockets and leaned her ass against a wall. "I like him. He's gentle, he's honest, and what he sees, he sees very clearly."

I said, "He's a retard. They've got papers on him."

"Maybe that's why I like him. Maybe I'm a retard, too. We can't all be as smart as you."

"Marry the bastard, have a couple of kids. If you're lucky, they'll take after their father."

She started to walk off but turned back. "I took him to a planetarium once. . . . I take him places. Did you know that?"

She knew I didn't.

"After the show, he asked me, 'If the stars are lights, what are they for?' "

It sounded like a crock of shit to me, and I said so.

"Everything sounds like a crock of shit to you," she snapped.

"Maybe that's because everything is."

No matter how slow he was, there were things you did not do to Frank, and surprising him was one of them. He'd tear off your head before he knew who you were. So when some of us on the shift got to playing practical jokes on each other, we left Frank out of it.

Surprise was the name of the game. I don't know how we got started, maybe it was all that empty space—but the point was to get a man alone and scare the shit out of him. Packager goes to storage for boxes. On his way back he walks by a forklift. Somebody jumps out from behind it screaming bloody murder. It was like laser tag without the technology. Anyway, it broke up the time.

Believe me, what the victim felt was not funny. You'd laugh later, but the scare would put the fear of God in a stone. When you walked through the warehouse at night, just you and the stacks and the rolls wrapped in plastic, your steps would sound ten times as loud as they should, and they'd echo. Suddenly there would be a movement behind you, a scream. Shit, you could paint the ceiling on the way down.

After a while, the game migrated onto the cutting floor, where it was mostly me and the packagers against the cutters. We'd do it with tape—a wide nylon packaging tape in a pistol dispenser. When you pulled it out fast, it sounded like ripping sheet metal. You'd sneak up on a cutter, who was concentrating on keeping his edges true, and tear off a screamer. He'd find out fast why he had those pedals.

It was Taylor I got to the most. He was such a nervous, prissy bastard, him and his thirty thousand yards. Some of the cutters developed a sixth sense for trouble, but when Taylor was concentrating on an edge, the fucking factory could burn down and he wouldn't notice. Rip one off behind him, and he'd howl and cuss and threaten to beat the tar out of you and report you to Ferris, all hundred and twenty pounds of him—still, you could stand behind him for half an hour and he'd never know you were there. Finally, with me, he just gave up. He'd cut the scrap out of the works and start over without even looking my way.

Me, I didn't have to deal with it that much. I could feel them coming. When I wanted to sleep, I'd go to ground in X-ray, the one place where no one could find me.

Even on swing shift, passing the X-ray door (which was only a cut in the wallboard with a knob attached) with the warning light above it, I'd wonder what went on inside. Rays that could see through to the bone. But you couldn't get in because the machine was running. So after they bumped me to nights, it was the first place that came to mind when I went exploring.

I followed a passage that doubled back and then doubled back again. There were no lights overhead, and black curtains blocked out what slivers of light might get in. In the coating room, the overhead lights cast a deep red glow. You had to wait for things to come clear, and they took their time. Then you could see the trays and the humpbacked coater and the curtained door on the other side where the tow motors brought in the rolls. Everything floated just under the surface of a pool of red water.

I loved that light. What it hit glowed, and what it missed wasn't there. The shadows were real, you couldn't see in. Since there were no in-between shades, there were no shapes. A barrel looked as flat as a tray. There was a black sludge of silver, thousands of dollars' worth, that slopped around in the bath, swaying in time with the vibration of the floor. I stumbled a lot at first, misjudging where the floor was. But I got used to the light and picked up the knack of walking in it. There was no yesterday, no tomorrow, in that room. Hassles went flat and floated away. I'd drag some wastepaper into the shadow of the machine and sleep.

Finally we called a halt to the games. One night, while I was listening to the rattle in a conveyor, Mr. Tattoo brought a crowbar down on the steel curb a couple of inches from my head, and later I got my revenge by shooting off a nail gun next to his ear, which ran a nail about five inches into his roll. That was as far as anybody wanted to take it.

And then Sandy came back. I woke up one evening, and she was standing at the foot of my bed. "Hello, asshole," she said.

Took about ten years off my life. Maybe I should've steered clear of her, but I was horny and it was free.

She wasn't the same. She looked older, uglier. The tough had worn thin, and you could see through it in places. She laughed a lot—a ticklish kind of laugh like a child's.

There were times when she'd lock her front door, and if you looked through a window, you could see her sitting with her knees drawn up, staring at nothing. Bang on the window and she'd turn her face to the wall.

You could tell the men were pissed off at her for coming back, but they left me alone. Naturally, Big Frank didn't catch on too quickly. I'd interrupt his heart-to-heart with Sandy to ask if there was any chicken left in her fridge, and he'd cover my shoulder with his paw and shake me, shouting, "Hey! Hey!" as if to say: Mind your manners.

Finally, an idea came oozing up out of the tar that maybe there was something between Sandy and me. Presto! Totally different moron. When he passed, he'd flash a big smile. Sometimes he'd grab my hand and pat it the way she did his. It got me so pushed out of shape, I had to soak up a dose of X-ray to get back my balance.

About once a month Frank's cutter would break down, and there'd go a couple of hours, when I was lucky. Ferris had given him the oldest machine in the factory, a belt-driven sheeter that looked like an old steel drawbridge and sounded like a hot time on a roll-away bed. It took the patience of a rock to run the damned thing, but when it was working, it put out sheets faster than an automatic. Parts weren't a problem—nothing wore out on it—but it had this complicated cut-and-feed action that went out of synch whenever a sheet got caught in the works.

While I was working on it, Frank would be huddled on his stool in agony. His machine, his fault—that's what he figured. When I finished, you'd think I had handed him the keys to a Mercedes. It would be all I could do to keep him from kissing me. But as soon as he connected me with Sandy, that changed. Now, he hung over my shoulder like a vulture, fingering the parts I laid on my cloth as if they were symbols in code.

I'd say, "Frank, go away."

And he'd answer, "Okay," but wouldn't move an inch. He'd just whisper to himself.

"How do you know how to fix things?" The way he asked it, you'd think I was Houdini or something.

"By not asking questions."

It was a dumb thing to say. As though he could pick up a hint. He toed a little pile of paper dust.

"I have to. It's the way I was born."

Even at lunch, I couldn't get rid of him. The niggers were sitting at the long table, so I took a table on the other side of the room. I'll work with them and I'll salute them, but I hate like hell to eat with them. It makes my food taste funny. Damned if Frank didn't pull out the chair next to me, "May I?" and drop into it like an avalanche before I could reply.

He arranged four milk cartons in a row, set a napkin in front of them, and stacked three sandwiches on top of it. Some of the men sat with the niggers, the rest someplace else. There was plenty of room. I was tempted to move, but I figured he would follow me.

Mr. Tattoo started riding me about my new buddy till I asked him, politely, how he'd like his ass nailed to a wall.

Frank tapped me on the wrist with a finger the size of a king snake and said, right out of the blue, "Do you believe in life after death?"

I said, "Shit, I'm not even sure the sun's coming up tomorrow."

"I am."

"Well, keep it to yourself. You'll have everybody believing it, and think how disappointed they'll be if it doesn't."

That seemed to worry him, the idea that people might follow his lead and regret it, sitting at their windows, waiting for the sun to rise. He ate real slow, leaning over his napkin, and when he finished the first sandwich he began to cry.

"My brother's dead."

"I heard."

"He was in the machine before it broke. He was flying."

I said, "Frank, if anybody got caught in there, they'd be chopped into confetti."

Son of a bitch looked at me like I was the moron.

"I know that. But I see things when the sheets go through. I see the ocean and my grandfather's farm, I see Sandy. I look at something and see something else. It's the way I am."

Telling me seemed to make him feel better. He ate the next sandwich in four bites and wiped his lips with the edge of the napkin.

"Dad says they'll come for me if I don't watch out, but he doesn't mean it."

I thought, if they ever do, I want a ringside seat. That'd be the fight of the century.

"But the things I see never stay the same. They change into other things." The tears returned. "I want them to stay the same."

I stuffed what was left of my lunch into the sack and tossed it at the can. It missed, but I figured the janitors needed the work.

"Dead's dead, Frank. There's nothing in that machine but paper."

He shook his head, and the tears kept coming.

On the cutting floor, I finally made him sit on his stool, but right away he clasped his hands together and prayed. Then he held them eye level and squinted into the gap between his thumbs. I thought, what now? A little while later he started talking, so low I couldn't make out the words. It scared me because I knew what he was saying had something to do with me.

When his machine was fixed, I said, "Get back to work."

His head came up slow. "If he's dead, how come I still see him?"

I tapped him upside the head with a ball of wastepaper.

"Something's wrong with the inside of your head, Frank. I mean, seriously wrong." He nodded, and a tear dribbled alongside his nose. I don't know what got into me, but I couldn't stop. I said, "The doctors ought to know what you're up to before it gets worse."

He gave out a groan you could hear across the river and rocked on his stool, pounding his head against an invisible wall, and it struck me that this guy could crack my skull with the back of one hand. But I kept going. I'd started to dump my load, and it had its own momentum.

"You've got problems, Frank. I mean, deep problems. They're going to take you to the hospital, give you some shocks before you get any worse."

"You don't know," he moaned.

"I know."

"How?"

"I was born knowing."

Stroke of genius. If I'd argued with the bastard, he never would have believed me, but being born knowing he could understand. His chin glistened like an icicle in the sun.

"Tell you what," I said. "I'll cut you a deal. You stay away from me, and I won't tell the doctors what I know. Okay?"

"Okay."

He stopped rocking and sat still, his face all crumpled, while I cleaned up my mess. Then he went back to work.

The rest of the night, he didn't come near me. He stood up straight over his machine—not checking for spots, not keeping the edges, just watching the blade rise and fall. At the end of the shift, Ferris had to throw most of it out.

I thought that was that, but I should've known better. You can't deal with them. They don't remember. You've got to pound a thing into their brains before it sinks in. The next night, I pushed through the turnstile and a shadow moved up behind me. It said, "What does dead mean?"

Scared the shit out of me.

I told him, "You sneak up on me again, you're going to find out."

"I'm sorry. I didn't mean to scare you." He reached out a hand as if he wanted to pet me, but I jumped out of the way.

Still, he didn't lay off. Every time a break rolled around, he'd be waiting. It got so that even the sight of him at his machine worried me. I'd start flashing on all kinds of shit, like somebody inside my head was throwing switches. I'd get hyper, and I'd fuck up what I was working on.

It didn't do any good to tell him to get lost. He'd always say, "Okay," and then stand there like a tree. Sooner or later he'd come out with whatever was on his mind.

"Do you think there's life on other planets?"

I said, "If there is, it probably looks like you."

But insults didn't work, either. Nothing worked.

At first, he'd only talk to me on break, and I could handle that, but after a while, he started tailing me. I'd be testing the hot wire on a packager, and out of the corner of my eye I'd catch a white smear slipping behind a pillar. Or I'd come out of the parts cage and see a pair of black pants behind a shelf full of barrels. Sometimes he'd be standing outside the john when I came out.

I'd say, "What are you after?"

But he wouldn't answer.

I got the feeling that if I ever picked up the telephone, my ass would be history.

I tried to tell Sandy to put a halter on him, but she thought the whole scene was hilarious. It wouldn't surprise me if she encouraged him.

He caught me one night coming out of X-ray and wouldn't let me pass. "Sandy says you lie."

"I don't lie, Frank."

"You do, too," like maybe he should rip out one of my arms.

"Then how come she sleeps with me, if I'm a liar?"

He knew what "sleeps with" meant, sort of, and it stopped him cold. He puzzled over it for the rest of the night.

A couple of days later, same place. "Do you love Sandy?"

I said, "Forget it, Frank."

He said, "What do you mean 'forget' ?"

"I don't know, just do it."

Then he got this enormous, shit-eating grin on his face and shouted—I mean, really shouted—"You don't know!" And poked a finger into my rib cage. One finger, and it bent me over double.

After that, I got me a thin piece of steel, wrapped one end in tape, and honed down the other—just in case. By the end of the week Frank was carrying one, too. Which really got me paranoid because you can never tell when a guy like that might look at you but see something else— something that needs its edges cut off.

In the lunchroom, there were more and more questions, only now they sounded like Frank's idea of a game. The kind a kid plays when he finds out "why" can go on forever. Frank would have his milk and his sandwiches out in battle lines in front of him, and the niggers would sit where they could watch. Most of the rest would be at the long table pretending to mind their own business, but when I walked in the room, the volume would drop. Soon, the questions would begin: What's an Arab? What's a revolution? Do you believe in God? Do you love Sandy? Do you have a brother? What happens when you're dead? One after the other, as if there was some crazy sequence that made sense to him.

Once in a while, I'd give him some bullshit answer. Mostly, I just ate.

It didn't matter what I did, sooner or later he'd yell, "You don't know!" Like that really put a cork in it, and from then on I'd know I was dealing with one smart moron.

The goons at my table always split a gut, and then Frank would light up and flap his hands together, which would set them off again. Meanwhile, I'd hear the home-boys jiving. I'd look around, and they'd all be smiling in my direction.

He kept it up for a week or more. What could I do? I could've eaten by myself, but then I'd look like a fool. I couldn't sabotage his machine, unless I wanted to put it together again. I couldn't fight him. There was one time when I did lose my cool, but he caught my fist in midair and tossed it back to me like a ball. Even in X-ray I couldn't get loose. I'd see those shadows moving and feel the way I did when that bag came up out of the river and tried to crawl back on land.

I went to Ferris and said, "Keep that fucker away from me. He follows me all over the plant."

He wheezed happily as if it was all a big joke.

I said, "Frank's got a knife."

He said, "So do you," and sighted me over the tip of his pen. "Frank mimics you. Don't ask me why, but he thinks you're special. He thinks you're his friend."

"But he's got to be away from his machine half the night."

Ferris picked a sheet out of the file and dropped it in front of me. "Two months ago, he was averaging 21,600 sheets; last week he averaged 23,200. If that's what happens to production when people chase you around the plant, I may form a posse."

"He's lying."

"Frank never lies. He doesn't know how."

"Look, I'm making a formal complaint. You can't sit there and do nothing."

The lowest drawer of his desk was pulled out. He propped his feet on it and leaned back. "Sure I can."

You see how it is. Doesn't matter if you follow the rules. They've got the power—Ferris and Woodall and the rest

—and if you're not their kind, they won't do shit for you. War games, again. They've got more guns, so they count on you backing down. But I'd done that once with Woodall, and once was about as much as I could take.

I was sitting at the long table with the three packagers, who liked me for the same reason that the cutters didn't: I was the one they blamed for the tape game. Old Frank thundered down right next to me, lined up his milks, unfolded his napkin, grinning as though he'd arrived where good morons go when they die. Taylor slid in across from him, said, "I'm behind," inhaled some soup, and poof! He was gone.

The packagers were trading glances because they weren't used to Frank up close. It was one thing to have a guy a couple of tables over, nodding and grinning and talking under his breath; it was another to have him crowding your space.

I said to the redhead, in front of Frank, "Let's play a joke on our buddy here. How about it?"

He said, "Sure." And the other two agreed. Then Frank said, "Sure," and we all busted out laughing.

After lunch, Frank went to wash his hands, and the four of us went for the tow motors. The cutters started their machines and then, one by one, shut them down again to see what we were up to. Soon there was only a couple going at the warehouse end of the floor, and Taylor's, which was not far from the john. Taylor glanced up when I passed by on the tow motor, but only for a second. He wasn't going to lose a roll on my account.

While we waited for Frank on our tow motors, the other two shut down and there was only the noise of Taylor's cutter, louder now for lack of competition. When Frank come out of the john, he stopped, listened, and then walked toward the sound.

The redhead turned into the aisle behind him, and the rest of us revved up. He didn't notice, not till he came to

the intersection next to Taylor's machine. Then he did a
full three-sixty like a dancing bear. Four lifts were coming
at him from opposite directions. You could see him trying
to puzzle it out, but he wasn't scared. You don't scare a
man that dumb very easy.

"Ride him in!" The redhead was standing up as he
drove, waving his free arm.

One of the others had a rope he was snapping in the
air. "Get along now. Get along."

I sounded my horn, and we raised the forks on our
machines. Then you could see the fear creeping in. Frank
kept turning around and around, his hands in front of
him. And Taylor's machine kept pounding.

I felt like a load had dropped from my shoulders. I
shouted, "Run him through!"

But the sound of my voice had a strange effect. The son
of a bitch turned toward me, his head cocked a little to
one side, a big grin on his face, the fear gone.

"Get him!" I cried, and he flapped his hands together,
applauding.

I could feel their eyes on me, everyone in the fucking
place watching.

"Get him!" My foot jammed down on the accelerator.

I didn't see what happened next. I felt the jolt that
stopped the motor and heard somebody scream. All I saw
was one of my forks about six inches from the redhead's
knee. I kept staring at that fork, and it didn't come to me,
at first, what I was looking for, just that it didn't look
right. Only when I backed away and saw Taylor and one
of the packagers trying to pull Frank out of the cutter did
I realize he'd jumped clear of me.

He was sobbing and didn't want to be lifted off. There
was blood spreading down the paper. They pried him
loose and sat him on the frame, trying to keep his right
hand up. I could see that two of his fingers were gone and
another one hanging from what looked like a bunch of

dirty white twine, blood spurting out of the stumps onto the floor. Taylor ran for an ambulance. The pill popper, blood all over his shirt, was trying to tie a tourniquet while the rest were holding Frank still. Under their feet, the paper dust made red clay out of the blood.

Then Frank saw me, pushed away the people that had hold of him, and shouted my name. I ran for my life—ran right past Ferris coming in, through the warehouse, out the gate, and when I climbed in my truck, I locked both doors.

I expected somebody to come after me, but nobody did. I drove home, fell into bed, and slept till one in the afternoon. When I woke up, I felt fine. All the shit from Bud and Sandy and the rest had washed away. I'd done what I had done, and it was over. I made myself some breakfast and ate it on the front stoop. The sun was hot and the trees had new leaves, and I could almost smell the steam from a wet spring forest drying.

In a way, I figured, Frank had it coming. Ferris could've stopped it. Anybody could've stopped it. But they figured if anybody got hurt, it would be me, so they egged him on. If it *had* been me, they would've probably thrown a party.

I took my tent and sleeping bag from the closet and aired them out, cleaned my guns, and slipped them into the rack behind the seat of the truck. Sandy came by to tell me they wanted me at the factory at five. She offered to drive. There wasn't much of hers at my place, but she made a big deal out of taking what there was. It surprised me that she never asked what had happened, but I expect she didn't want to hear an answer any more than I wanted to give one.

Sometime after five I walked into the foreman's office —where Frank and Ferris and Woodall and Taylor and the redhead were standing with some office types and these two guys in suits with lumps under their jackets. I figured either they were cops or they weren't long for this world. Frank's right eye had closed, and the whole right side of his face was swollen, which made him look even more like one of those fat Buddhas. He had to tip his face to the side like a bird to look at me, and he kept picking at the bandages that covered his stumps till he got them bleeding again. It made me sick to watch.

You could tell who was in charge. He was black and the only man in a vest, and you could tell *he* thought Frank was one of them.

"The men say you engineered this."

"It was a joke," I said. "He panicked."

"I don't know anyone who considers assaulting a man with a forklift funny."

I didn't answer, just stared at him until he looked away. I said, "It was an accident."

"Come off it! Winslow Taylor saw everything. He tells me you shouted, 'Get him!' Several times. It was you who forced Mr. Hooker to jump. You came at him with the fork of your tow motor raised."

I said, "I wouldn't hurt Frank. Frank's my buddy. Anyway, if Taylor saw the whole thing, how come he didn't stop his machine? All he had to do was lift his foot off the pedal."

"How could I know?" Taylor shouted. "How could anybody know . . ." He couldn't finish, he was so pissed.

One of the cops broke in. He was tall and thin and had this little blond mustache. "None of this matters. The real question is, why did you speed up when the rest of them had stopped? It wasn't an accident. You came at him so fast, you damaged the machine you ran into."

"My foot slipped."

"Your foot slipped." He said it slow between his teeth. "There isn't a man on God's earth who'd believe your foot slipped!"

Frank said, "I do."

The cop was so surprised, I don't think he realized at first who had said it. Then you should have seen his face.

"Mr. Hooker, this isn't the time to make statements."

But Frank didn't listen. "He's my friend. He talks to me."

"Frank." The three-piece suit held out his hand. He might as well have tried to stop a bullet with it.

"I don't see things right. It's the way I was born," Frank continued.

The three-piece suit looked at the cop, who said, "Later." Then he turned to me. "Don't come back."

I said, "Fine."

"If you ever set foot on this property . . ."

"When do I get my paycheck?"

That floored him. He just stood there and twitched. Finally he said, real soft, "I'll have it mailed."

I turned to leave, feeling like I'd just raked in an armful at Vegas, and there's Frank behind me looking sad the way he did when he talked about his brother, and it hit me that he knew the truth. Even with one good eye and his face as swollen as it was, you could tell that he knew, and that whatever he wanted to do, nobody was going to stop him. Grabbing my arm, he brought his face down close to mine, to where I could feel his breath, and my breakfast came up in my mouth.

But all he did was rub that stump against my cheek as if he was trying to pet me. The bandage was still wet, and I could feel the blood on my face; the smell of it made me dizzy. Then he let me go.

Sandy was waiting outside. "They didn't arrest you?" She sounded disappointed.

That night I had a headache, big-time. Like somebody'd set a wedge right down the middle of my skull and was

pounding it in. And there was rain, lots of rain, and that
god-awful smell came up from the basement. After the
storm had passed, I fell asleep, and for the first time in
years, I dreamed.

I saw myself running through a forest, and people were
chasing me, I could hear their footsteps, but they kept
hidden. Which didn't make sense because the trees were
tall and there wasn't much cover. Now and then I'd see
shadows moving, but every time I aimed my rifle, they
disappeared. This went on and on, and I got more and
more tired because I couldn't take the chance of stopping.

Then we were in the warehouse among the plastic-
covered rolls, but the lights were red like the ones in X-
ray. I was trapped. The doors were locked, and the man
with the tattoos was waiting at the entrance to the cutting
floor, when suddenly they showed themselves. They rose
up from behind the rolls. The nigger in the vest was one
of them—the rest I didn't know. They all had guns, but
they just stood there. Then I saw Frank. He had torn off
his bandages, and was coming down the aisle, calling my
name. As his T-shirt settled under my sights, I felt this
incredible rush and pulled the trigger—five or six times,
as fast as I could—but nothing happened. I could feel his
hands grab hold of me, I could smell the blood on my
face.

I woke up breathing hard and spent the rest of the night
watching lights play across my ceiling and wondering
where they came from.

The next morning, I found the driver's-side window on
my truck smashed, but still together. I couldn't find what
they used, and I couldn't get it down. It just hung there all
in pieces, yellow in the yellow light, like a stained glass
sunburst. I thought of the guy with the tattoos, I thought
of Sandy, but hell, it could've been anybody. I went back
for my .357 and shoved it under the seat.

I stopped at a diner for breakfast, took my money out

of the bank and kited checks for supplies. Every time I
tried to look through that window, I wanted to shove a
tire iron down somebody's throat. Shapes were all jumbled up. Colors moved, but you couldn't tell what they
were, or where.

By the time I got home, my head was pounding so bad,
I threw up, which helped some. I lay down and slept until
evening, but when I woke, there they were—the shadows
rising up from behind the rolls like an army of niggers,
Frank's stump on my cheek and the smell of blood. The
phone rang. I ripped it out of the wall. The headache was
gone, but my body felt heavy, and I kept running into
things like a drunk. I packed my gear under a tarp in the
truck but couldn't decide where to go. The road atlas was
nothing but lines—blue lines and red lines and black
lines, crisscrossing like cracks in dry ground—with
splotches of color underneath. It made me tired just to
look at them.

I got in the truck and drove past Sandy's house. It was
dark, and the car was gone. I parked in a McDonald's lot
a couple of blocks away, jumped a fence, and let myself
in with a crowbar. Dirty dishes were in the kitchen sink,
pipe tobacco in an ashtray. Her clothes were gone, along
with some things she had hanging on the walls and her
checkbooks. The bathroom still smelled of perfume. I cut
up the bed, pulled out the stuffing, and spread it around,
and when I finished, I had this incredible hard-on. Some
cops crawled by in a squad car and flashed a spot on the
house, but they didn't see me.

I headed in the direction of the railroad depot, where
the faces were black and the storefronts were soaped
white. The dusk like smoke in my lungs. They were hanging out everywhere, on street corners and porches, in
front of caged liquor stores and pawnshop churches. I
thought how easy it would be to waste a couple of dozen,
if you didn't mind going down with them.

Across the track was the factory, lit up like a prison yard, and beyond it the river snaked along. I must've driven by five or six times, not knowing what to do, wishing I could get hold of some dynamite. Three teenagers that looked as if they'd been sleeping in a dumpster somewhere stood across from the gates outside the video store and every time I went by one of them would slouch toward the curb. I thought, Shit. Why not?

So I stopped, and a boy opened the door of the truck. He wore slick black shorts, a white T-shirt, and grinned like a kid getting a carnival ride. He said, "Twenty?"

I said, "Sure."

When he closed the door, you could smell him. You wonder how they make any money stinking like that.

I took him along the river road and after we drove out past the houses, I pulled the pistol from under my seat. "Guess what? It's your day to die."

He held out his hands, palms up. "I don't have any money."

"I don't give a shit about money."

The smile stayed stuck to his face as though someone had nailed it on. "Why?"

"For the fun of it." I pulled off into the trees behind a burnt-out house.

It was quiet. You could hear the river slapping the shore. I got some rope from the back and herded the boy through the underbrush. In the moonlight, the bright spots seemed higher than the shadows, and we stumbled a lot, both of us. By the time we reached the water, he could barely walk. I figured on scaring him a little and leaving him tied up in the dark, but while I was binding his hands, he said, "This is stupid." And it pissed me off.

I took the butt of the gun and beat the shit out of his face. "Is that stupid? How about that?" Till he stopped screaming and started crying.

He lay in a patch of moonlight, with his face buried in

trash that the river had washed up, whispering, "Please, please," through the blood in his mouth. I let him feel the gun at the back of his head, then moved it away a little and pulled the trigger. It made a big hole in the mud, but he didn't even flinch.

There's an expression that an animal gets when it's been wounded but can't run away—like it's looking at a tree at the edge of the universe. Sometimes you walk up to them and they don't even turn their heads. That's what happened to this kid. I put the gun between his eyes, and he stared right through it. So I left him there.

I drove all night and all the next day, eating candy bars and drinking tequila, and finally pulled into a motel some-place where there was lots of corn and people who looked like they belonged in it. Two days later I was where I'd started, in the middle of the Idaho wilderness —clean air and nobody for miles.

Yet nothing's changed. I walk and walk, but it's like walking in place, and all around me the shadows are moving. I can't hunt. I put my eye to the scope, but I can't make any connection between what I saw just before and what's there in the lens. Scares the shit out of me. I'll squeeze off a burst just to be sure the rifle's not jammed.

At night, zipped in my bag, I stare up at the stars as if from the bottom of a river—sleep and wake, sleep and wake, listening to the forest—and I can feel myself shrinking and the stars getting farther away, like if I laid there real quiet I might disappear.

Someone Else

J E W S moved into the house where Amy Richardson had died, and that created a predicament. All week long Naomi Wheelock watched them from the antique-cluttered front room that had once been her husband's study and wondered, without malice, why people will not stay with their own. Saturday morning, while her son was out shopping, she made up a basket of gourmet tins from S. S. Pierce, including a jar of her own plum preserves, and, after some consideration, added a "Welcome" note and signed it "Mrs. Naomi Wheelock and Lewis Wheelock." It was the most that could be expected of her, she thought, and left the basket on the kitchen table for Lew to take over.

But when Lew returned he was still under a cloud (the Flores woman had phoned that morning). One look at the note, and he flew into a pet, pacing before the stove with his hands in his pockets.

"Why do you always put me in this position?"

Lew always made a fuss about being consulted. She watched him, bobbing as he complained: an adenoidal old maid, not five feet two, trying to ride his father's high horse.

"There is nothing wrong with common courtesy," she said.

Her son gripped the edge of the sink and glared at the herbs in tiny plastic pots along the windowsill. "When they drop by to return your courtesy and you're suddenly taken ill, who'll have to stand at the door making excuses?"

She lifted her bulk slightly and resettled it on the wooden kitchen chair. "Would you rather I snubbed them?"

Lew thought, yes, at least everyone would know where they stood, but he could tell from her lady-of-the-manor tone that it was useless to argue. She'd tell him her gift

was insignificant, but that such things mattered a great
deal to her. If he still didn't go, she'd sulk for weeks.
At eighty-seven, she would probably never accept that
the days of elegant prejudice were over, when a gesture
like this defined social distances rather than bridging
them.

And, much as he hated playing errand boy for his mother's fantasies, Lew had to admit that he'd begun to sym-
pathize with some of the old-fashioned properties she
displayed, like her Edward VI coronation china, behind
locked glass doors. In the end, he thought, everyone had
a right to a corner of the world where reality did not
contradict them.

The Wheelock house was three doors up from the intersection of Blackstone and Hyde, near a small and still
fairly exclusive shopping district in the suburb of Newton.
Blackstone beveled off this crossroad at a weird angle,
curved toward the house below theirs, then climbed
three-quarters of the way up a steep hill, swung a languid
U, and switchbacked down to Hyde again. It was a turn-
of-the-century street lined with broad two- and three-
story frame houses that, according to one of Lew's less
reverent brothers, hadn't the nerve to be mansions. The
street required *knowing*—how to enter a driveway, step
off the curb without stumbling—and as Lew crossed it,
he enjoyed the sense of being at home. The neighborhood
had changed, but not as drastically as the city. He tried to
imagine what it might be like to move from this place,
where he had spent all of his forty-eight years, to another,
where he would walk like a lame man. He was reminded
of the Italian gardener who'd worked for them when his
father was alive, a man bent by constant labor, begging
pardon for the slightest mistake. What could be so impor-
tant to a man that he would exile himself?

The house the Jews bought had remained vacant for
two years after Miss Richardson's death while a court

decided the legality of her bequest to a nephew. Already
the owners had repaved the drive, and there were blocks
of shingles in plastic shrink wrap stacked along the side
yard. The spongy new asphalt gave pleasantly under
Lew's tread. Toward the back of the house a man on the
third section of an aluminum ladder was doing something
to a gutter pipe. But the first step on the porch stairs still
had that soft plank. The same rusted doorbell he'd
pressed as a child sounded the same asthmatic burr inside. He hoped they would leave that alone, at least, as a
legacy of what had come before them.

The door was open a crack, but he let it be and glanced
at the contents of the basket—four cans and a jar. Obviously a conscience offering. Meant to be obvious, he
thought. Anger rose as a thin, sharp pain in his belly but
disappeared the moment he noticed it. Inside he could
see the bottom post of the scrolled balustrade over which
Miss Richardson had taken to leaving her coat during the
last year of her life. (Hearing of this, his mother had pre-
dicted her death.) Somewhere beyond the hall an uneasiness swelled in the air, became a song:

> something, something
>
> His name it was Chris
> and the last was Magill
> I met him one night
> pickin' flowers on the hill
>
> La la la la la la
> and a certain kind of touch
> and a certain kind of eagerness
> that pleased me very much

The door vanished, and in its place stood a beautiful
dark-haired woman in a red work shirt, smiling down at
him as he held out the basket. She squinted against the

glare, at the gray stubble atop his head, at the glasses slipped halfway down his nose. The usual pleasantries stuck in his throat; they seemed, in her presence, contemptible. The curve of her cheek filled him with apprehension, urged him to flee—*Sorry, I seem to have made a mistake*—to lie, to pretend to be someone else, and his voice stalled like a flooded engine.

The woman laughed. "Hi, there! You're from across the road?"

His eyes dropped to the delta at the base of her neck. "Yes," he said.

"I'm Evelyn Weiss. Oh, what's this? Goodies!" She held out her hands like a child.

"Mother," he explained, "wanted you to have—"

"Herring! I'll have to hide it from Dulcy. Brown bread! How nice. You must thank your mother for me. I was beginning to think no one gave a damn. Grape?"

"Plum."

"Blintzes, definitely. We haven't had anything but that store muck for ages. Do you like blintzes?"

The pressure of the basket against her chest bunched her shirt and revealed a slim blade of flesh between the second and third buttons. He looked away.

"I'm sorry if I seem startled," he apologized. "I expected someone older."

"You *are* a dear. And me pawing through the goods like a schnorrer. Won't you come in? I've got some coffee on. It'll give me an excuse to get Alex off that ladder. Dulcy's —I don't know where Dulcy is. . . . Dulcy?"

"No, don't," he pleaded. "Another time, please. When you're settled."

"Okay, but it's a date. Bring your mother and whoever, and we'll have a feast. I'm a damned good cook when I want to be."

His head drooped. "Mother doesn't go out, except to visit family," he said quietly. "She's very old. This is the best she can do."

The woman surprised him by showing concern. "That's too bad. I'll have to stop by. Are you married?"

"No."

"Got a girl?"

"Sort of." He smiled uncomfortably.

"Bring your girl. A couple of Alex's mai-tais and she won't be 'sort of' anymore. Believe me, I speak from experience. Soon?"

"Yes, soon," he sighed.

The vapor of fresh asphalt had staled in his mouth, and of course there was no liquor in the house, no cigarettes, no magazines beyond *National Geographic,* and no music since Gilbert and Sullivan. Lew recalled his father, thumb caught in his vest, back to the fireplace, reviewing the highlights of his day at St. John's Masonic Temple. Grand Secretary General of the Free and Accepted, his father had believed quite sincerely that he was the keeper of a sacred light. He'd stand before the fire, examining his children, drawing lessons in the air with two fingers outstretched like the legs of a compass—vessels of body and streams of mind. As if the two were not bound together with cables of steel.

Lew reached between the cartons of milk and grapefruit juice and pried a can of Dr. Pepper from its plastic cuff. In the chromed freezer door, a pink globe rose as he rose; a frown he hadn't felt reflected back at him, bunched over black glasses; his mouth was pinched by a dent in the door he'd made four or five years ago, the night Ruth wept over a thirty-dollar steak and called him niggling. *Niggling*—what a strange word. The maître d' had put a hand on her shoulder and asked if there were something wrong with the meat, which made her laugh and choke on her tears. Lew grimaced at the apparition in the chrome, and it grimaced back. The door closed of its own momentum.

The clocks needed winding—that was essential—then perhaps he'd clean the fish pond. He rolled the icy can over his forehead to stanch the last traces of heat.

"Two-ish," Ruth had said. It had been an awkward phone call. She'd asked how he was and babbled something about being sorry. There'd been concern in her voice, and excitement.

Lew thought of the Jewish woman. The stuttering fool he'd been had disappeared from memory, leaving only the image of her beauty and charm.

He lifted a necklace of keys from the nail above the phone and dug out a three-step ladder from the hall closet. The toilet flushed in the half bath he'd built off the study. He opened the ladder beside a black grandfather clock that guarded the foot of the stairs and unlatched the face from the second step. This was a cheap one; the numerals were painted on the window. He fit his first hollow key into a slot below the hour hand and wound.

Naomi Wheelock emerged from the study, slightly flushed, trailing essence of pine. She rested a hand against the side of the clock for balance.

"Well? Did you leave it on the doorstep?"

"I gave it to Mrs. Weiss. She was delighted."

"My goodness. And she didn't kick you down the stairs?" Savoring his silence, Naomi humphed good-humoredly. "You make too much of commonplaces."

Lew opened the pendulum door and began setting the weights—bland steel cylinders, baton-shaped. Concentrating on the chains, he recalled the expressionless stone that had been his mother's face before his father died. Now, it was happy, doughy, mobilized by a playfulness that he could not remember having seen before and found vaguely threatening. "She invited us to dinner when they get themselves arranged. I said yes—for myself."

"Obviously," Naomi said, but there was something plaintive in her retort.

"I told her you rarely go out and entertain only old friends. So she's going to stop by and thank you herself."

"Dear God. Why did you give her an explanation?"

"Convenience."

The curve of her back acquiesced, and as if he were counterpoised, Lew stood straight again.

"I'll be in my room lying down," she said.

Up the stairs she toiled, pausing at each step to hook her hand over the banister and draw herself to the next, a milkweed fluff of white hair floating above a wash-faded dress. Her son, watching, imagined the stair turning, catching her feet, escaping. He felt no affection. The stone had disappeared too late. Whistling the tune the Jewish woman had sung, he carried the open ladder into the living room.

Years ago, this room had been imposing in a large-family way. The Persian rug was now worn in spots, and the long velour couch had a spring loose; but, Naomi would remind him, the rug had cost $2,500 at 1947 prices, and the couch was one of a kind. Everything his mother owned was one of a kind, with the result that nothing had been added or removed in twenty years, and lately a mustiness had invaded the room. It had begun to stink, delicately, of wool in wet weather, and no amount of cleaning could get rid of the odor. Yet she wasn't aware of it, any more than she noticed the sourness of her own body.

Between the front windows and the fireplace, above shelves of books that no one, to his knowledge, had ever read, hung a banjo clock from E. Howard & Sons: a hand-tooled mahogany case, black-and-gold trim on the glass of the pendulum window (the bob appearing and disappearing like the moon behind a cloud), a quiet bell chime, and a simple enamel face with the barrel square at three and the chime at nine. Lew resisted the urge to stand on the bench of his mother's Steinway instead of the ladder. It occurred to him as he climbed toward the clock's face that Mrs. Weiss would not need a ladder. The barrel

wound smoothly with a purring of small teeth turned
back on their pawl.

Through a doorless portal, flanked by pre–Sun Yat-sen
Chinese pennants, he entered a small, liberally windowed dining room made almost impassable by a massive
oak table and chairs, set slightly off-center to accommo-
date the cabinet containing Naomi's crystal collection; it
was the brightest room in the house. The table, which
was capable of seating eight without leaves, had been set
for two, in keeping with her habit of setting for the next
meal after the dishes from the last had been washed. His
father had liked to see plates on the table waiting. Lew
remembered him sitting in the black leather chair in the
living room until the scattershot chimes announced six,
though never quite in unison, whereupon he would fold
his paper into the magazine rack, straighten his tie, and
stroll to his place at the head of the table. He didn't consider it necessary to ask his wife if dinner were ready. It
was six o'clock, dinner was served.

Lew glanced at the place he was expected to occupy
tonight and opened the case of a silent presentation
banjo. There were two clocks in the dining room: the
banjo to tell time and, to amuse his mother, an eccentric
Pennsylvania grandfather with a gong that could be heard
from the road. Apparently begun as an ordinary tall
clock, the latter had been finished, probably at the buy-
er's insistence, with a crudely carved border of snaking
vines and painted museum-frame gold. Her hobgoblin
clock, she called it. It had been left behind by the pre-
vious owner and placed here over his father's strenuous
objections. Naomi used to enjoy bringing small children
in to poke their fingers through the vines, making up stories about the ghost in the box and giggling at their
shrieks when it struck the hour.

It was hell to set: out of revenge, he suspected, the
clock maker had put the slot for the striking mechanism

on top. Standing on tiptoe, Lew reached over a mantrap of sharp wooden finials and groped for the hole. Once in a while the pawl would freeze. Eight days would blur past in five seconds; the weights would break loose and end up coiled among their chains at the bottom of the box like hanged men cut free. Today he was lucky—no trouble with the key, and his drop of the bob was perfect. He took it as a good omen. Before he went upstairs, he put away the plate, silver, and napkin reserved for him.

On the second floor he worked quickly, down one side of the corridor and back up the other, listening to the *telop-telop* of his footsteps on the wooden floors, the rattle of chains and winding mechanisms, the dull echo of his breath borne and swallowed by empty rooms. He passed his mother's door twice, glimpsed her yellow-brown feet on the white bedspread. If she heard him, she said nothing. And neither did he.

On the third, he breathed easier. The rooms were smaller and the head-high wainscoting shrank to ankle size: these were the servants' quarters, when they'd had servants, and a nursery. He and his brother Mark had lived here with a nanny whom he remembered simply as warmth and a musky smell. When his sister, Abby, had married, Mark as the elder had taken her room and left Lew to himself—the nanny, by that time, had gone. Now there wasn't much furniture: bureaus and box-spring beds with pinstripe mattresses, steamer trunks, and his father's gun collection in the servants' rooms; an old crib, a fireplace, and Lew's tall clock in the nursery.

Following his weekly routine, Lew opened the spigots in the bathroom and flushed the toilet a couple of times to keep rust out of the pipes. No one was going to use them, but a man had to maintain what was his, or would be.

"You should leave that mausoleum before they bury you in it," Ruth had protested.

But Ruth always came around eventually. It was natural
that a woman without a family, who had spent her life in
apartments, would see only a desert of empty rooms, for
she lacked the emotion of ownership. It took time to feel
a house in your bones, and even more until the sound and
touch and scent of possession fit over the senses like a
second skin.

"Don't you see how she's controlling you?" Ruth said.
"Sweet Christ, Lew, if you don't escape, there won't be
anything left of you to enjoy it."

Toweling his hands with brisk strokes, Lew walked into
the nursery to admire his handiwork. In a dark corner,
the English tall clock stood in its case of Yankee walnut.
He had built the case from scratch, working off and on
for over a year; he'd finished it a month ago, but Ruth had
yet to see it. He gazed into the dark-veined wood as
though he were looking for his face among the rings.

He'd told Ruth to go to hell. What right did she have, a
spinster librarian with a fear of heights, hiding in the
stacks from boys with knives? What did she know about
family? Her mother had died in an asylum. He contemplated in the wood the ironies of their fight: because she
had been right, he insulted her; and because he had
touched on the truth, she threw him out. Soon, they
would swear they hadn't meant the things they so obviously had, and if the wounds chafed, they'd tell each
other how much they had learned.

He hoped she wouldn't force him to play the romantic:
*I love you, you make life worth living, if you ever leave
me, I'll throw myself into the Charles.* Wasn't it sufficient
to say, "We're good friends and comfortable together?"

The memory of a sliver of flesh between black buttons
set his hands to wadding the towel, then faded, leaving a
backwash of resignation. Lew imagined running his finger
along the scar at the base of Ruth's neck, and his hands
clenched into fists. She was afraid it disfigured her, and

he was often forced to reassure her that it was nothing. But the thought of touching it repelled him.

He ran his fingertips lightly up the side of the case and rubbed them against his palm. The oil had begun to bleed a little—a natural consequence of the late spring heat.

Stored since the year of his father's death, victim of dry rot and his mother's refusal to let it out of the house for rebuilding, the clock, for Lew, had been a challenge in carpentry: to turn a decaying square-hooded Englishman into a flamboyant Yankee, hoisting a single finial like a flag through its broken pediment. Time and labor had made it an emblem of his creative powers, a sample of what he might do with the entire house someday. Of course, now that he had finished restoring it, his mother wanted it back, but he hadn't found the time to move it downstairs into that indiscriminate clutter of antiques and junk, nor would he in her lifetime.

A ring of pewter was welded to a disk of brass, and the brass was etched in an acanthus design. He dug a fingernail along the edge of the ring and hummed at the black line it left. Brass numbers gleamed against the gray. Above the squares the maker had etched "Westminster 8-chime, Jenness and Sons, London." He wound the barrel but not the chime—no need to remind her of it—and noticed that the sound was not as smooth as that of the Howard banjo clock, more like a rapid beat of wings. The weights were twice as heavy as any in the other clocks, squat cylinders of brass on brazen chains. The chimes were also brass and had begun to discolor. He'd have to spend an evening cleaning them and wiping the oil from the wood. Finished, he stepped back, fascinated by the easy swing of the grid pendulum. As with most good pendulums, the ellipsis was obvious and seemed irregular. Outside, the cries and catcalls of children were counterpointed by the thump of a soccer ball.

He smiled at the thought of the *tick-tock* fakery of the

tiny pendulum clock in Ruth's kitchen, a charming little bargain at double the value. "I have a feeling for it," she sniffed, which probably meant the salesman had bullied her. Mother with her freaks, and Ruth with her fakes. A rapid tattoo of kicks ended in a shriek of pain, shouts of "out" and "foul." Lew draped his towel over the porcelain rod, shut the cocks on the sink and tub, then discovered his towel was in a heap on the floor.

"Damn!"

He carefully folded the towel back over the rod.

Below, a burst of cheers had died suddenly, and one of the children shouted, "I'll get it!" He looked out the window expecting to find them fighting over the ball in his flower beds, but they'd lodged it in a spruce at the other end of the Cavanaughs' property. There were six of them around the tree—three Cavanaughs and three of unknown origin. The baby of the family, Kevin, was watching the others from a distance. Sooner or later they'd lob it over the hedge. Even if he lectured them, in ten minutes they'd be in his yard again. The Lew of thirty-five or forty would have laughed and kicked the ball back, but his knees had lost their resiliency, and his tolerance for childish mayhem had gone with it.

At the head of the stairs he stopped, but heard only the drone of a truck climbing up Blackstone. The silent house breathed with him and waited to be filled by the sound of his footsteps descending.

Pine scent still hung in the hall, and in the kitchen muffled thuds from the soccer game mimicked the throb in his ears. Raising his hand to stifle a cough, he saw a red-tipped fetus where his thumb should have been. "Damn her," he whispered. What melodrama would Ruth drag him through to make him pay for her return? He thought of Evelyn Weiss with his mother's basket cradled in her arms, and her husband on the third extension scooping leaves from the gutter—bald as an egg and beer-bellied.

On the back porch, the must of the house and the pun-
gent green of the garden mingled, their odors reminding
him of compost after a turning. A rake he'd left by the
door last weekend had fallen across the padded lounge,
etching a white flame into the dust. Near it were flats of
phlox and nemophila, which ought to be planted today
but wouldn't. He picked up the rake from the floor and
carried it out with him. One of the children, a girl he'd
never seen before, belly-flopped through the hedge and
nearly rolled down into his yard. Bounding up, she fought
her way back through the hedge screaming, "Fuck you,
faggots!" Nine, maybe ten years old. He shook his head.

In the garage he exchanged the rake for a rusty one
more suitable for combing plants out of the fish pond.
(Unusual for the lilies to spread as fast as they had, but it
had been a warm spring.) He surveyed with pleasure the
tools and implements hanging like pictures from hooks in
the walls: the lathe, the workbench, the stainless-steel
cabinet full of drawers. It took a long time for a man to
organize things so that he could reach into a drawer and
know, without looking, the size of the nail he would find.
To him, the geography of objects mattered far more than
romance. Passion was a violent and aimless energy; when
it decayed, as it always did, a comfortable order of things
took its place. Ruth could not comprehend this, but then
Ruth still expected a knight in shining armor to ride into
the public library and ask for the medieval history section.

Not that he hadn't had his struggles. How long had it
taken him to accept that the women he met in hotel
rooms solved only the momentary perplexities; that reality for him was a pale, gawky frame of edges and absences, cable-thin arms that frayed into fingers, and the
startled expression of a lost child? He didn't love her, no
one could. Nor could any sensible woman love the image
he'd seen on the freezer door. But he and Ruth had been

friends for eight years, and despite its turbulence, their friendship was solid. It was a thing he could take for granted, like the angle of Blackstone Street.

By the time he returned to the yard, the sounds of the game had ceased, and the explanation lay floating in the fish pond, a slick black-and-white nub on the scalelike skin of the lilies. He dredged it out with the rake and dropped it on the lawn. Boston Irish. They were worse than the blacks, almost. The next time he met Martin Cavanaugh, he intended to say, "How would you feel if I tossed my superfluous nymphaea on your living room floor?" And Mr. Cavanaugh, ignoring the sarcasm as he always did, would complain that none of his children were any good and Lew had been smart to remain a bachelor.

Predictably, the kids had sent Kevin after the ball. Lew watched as he stumbled down the slope of the terrace and shuffled sulkily to the pond, head hanging, a swatch of belly showing between his shirt and jeans. The boy gazed uncomfortably, first at the ball, then at Lew, as if the fact that Lew had retrieved it made him unsure of his right to pick it up.

"It's my brothers'. We were playing soccer," he said in two quick bursts, glancing up the hill.

"Go ahead."

It took the boy two tries to pick it up, and then he just stood there, holding it out in front of him so he wouldn't get wet.

"Kevin?"

"It was them, Mr. . . . . " The little face tightened in alarm. He'd forgotten the name.

"Go on," Lew sighed. "Tell your brothers that next time I keep the ball."

Kevin stayed where he was. Tears trailed down his cheeks.

"Goddamn it!" Lew reached out to give him a push, but

the boy shied away and scrambled frantically up the incline, wailing as though he'd been hit. Lew flung down the
rake and glared at the dark hole in the lily pads. He remembered Ruth's gaze falling to her lap, where her fingers had been weaving and unweaving patterns for more
than an hour.

"So what?" she had said. "You haven't changed, I
haven't changed, and so where are we? Are we actually
sitting in my apartment again, with glasses of wine, talking about our 'relationship'? Or is this yesterday? Or five
years ago? I can't tell anymore. We're drifting, Lew. We
always have, and I'm tired of it. You were wonderful
when I was afraid, but I don't want to be afraid anymore,
and you're satisfied with this."

Her gesture swept across a roomful of cozy furniture
and decorations ordered from catalogs, a bookshelf of
antique dolls, and an old Siamese cat who followed her
fluttering hand with predatory eyes. The gesture complete, her hand retreated self-consciously to worry a button at her breast. His eyes followed the scar's white ridge
to where it burrowed beneath her blouse.

"What do you want?"

"I want to do things."

"Like?"

Ruth nodded, as if that were the sort of reply she'd
expected.

He set his glass carefully onto the coaster. "I'm not a
mind reader, Ruth. Tell me what you want, and I'll do
what I can."

Laughter folded her like a jackknife, then burst out,
skidding wildly around the room, rising finally in a great
gasp, which trembled for an instant, then shattered into
giggles and snorts and subsided into shivering, wide-eyed
fury. She minced the words acidly. "An orgy, my dear.
Half a dozen men and a case of champagne, and a video
camera to record it all. See what you can do."

Two large goldfish mouthed curiously at the gap. Lew waved, and one of them dove. The other, imperturbable, calmly swallowed an insect. Behind him, he could hear his mother's hobgoblin clock striking one.

Naomi let her feet hang over the edge of the bed and, using them as a counterweight, pushed herself up with her elbows until she could use both hands, pressing down as hard as she could while a chill shook her and the patches of darkness faded from sight; then she let herself down. The ache began when her feet touched the floor. Odd to be able to feel the pain so distinctly when she could barely feel her feet. Across the hall she heard her son flustering about, primping himself for that tragic creature with the Spanish name. As she looked out the window, her mind slipped away. When it returned, she found herself staring at a strip of gray sunlight on the sash.

Lew was knotting his tie in front of the mirror as she entered. He allowed her a curt little nod.

"Have a good nap?"

From the way he ducked his head, she assumed he must be hiding something.

"Good enough," she said.

Inevitably, when he pulled up on the knot, the narrow end hung a couple of inches below the wide. Neither he nor his father could tie a tie properly in her presence.

"Here, let me."

He glowered at the suggestion and made a pout of forbearance toward some imaginary audience, but he obeyed. Children needed their pride, she supposed, even old children. His father had never minded.

"How do you feel?" Lew asked.

"Nothing serious, just a touch of diarrhea. If you could pick up some Pepto-Bismol on the way home . . ."

"I'll be late."

"Better late than never. Tomorrow is Sunday, you know. See? Nothing to it."

The wide edge drew out perfectly one inch below the narrow.

"Give Ruth my best," she added.

Following him to the head of the stairs, Naomi watched her son descend, running a hand over his liver-spotted scalp and slapping his pockets. She heard him whistle a rather graceless tune as he pitter-patted down the corridor, all for a pencil-thin neurotic who took pills to keep her hands from trembling.

Fool.

Traffic was unusually light on the freeway into the city. Lew tried to plan what he would say, but his nerves wouldn't let him. As the suburbs curved to a point in the center of his rearview mirror and disappeared, a kind of panic set in, as if he'd been trapped by a current in the middle of the river. Details of the passing scene—a billboard, an odd bit of architecture on a dilapidated house —beckoned to him like hands attempting to pull him to safety. Coming up behind a slow truck, he had to shift lanes to avoid the sudden terror of being sucked under. In the ebb of his fear, he saw Ruth—a younger Ruth— walking to her car after a movie. Three boys crossed the street in front of her. They were laughing and jostling one another as they approached. One tore her purse from her shoulder, another mauled her from behind. She screamed, faces turned, a man shouted, "Hey!" The boy who held her warned her to shut up, but the screams would not stop. Then the third, the smallest, took out a knife.

Off the freeway, Lew breathed easier. Through a shopping area below Chestnut Hill, he was stopped by a glut

of double-parked cars and a mad hunt for parking spaces
that crossed lanes and sides of the road and accelerated
through yellow lights. The delay gave him a chance to
wipe his sweaty hands on his pants and look around.

A fat man, his shirt mottled with sweat, stacked or-
anges in a trough outside a grocery; beside him, picking
through the cherries, stood a slim, stylish woman
wrapped in swirls of black and white that twisted like
flames toward her neck. Turned slightly from one another, their backs formed a wedge on either side of the
fruit scales. An enterprising dog trotted past, peeing on
every parking meter he encountered. The jam eased, and
Lew managed to slip into the left-hand lane and turn just
before the light changed.

The road climbed for several blocks between sedate
wine-brick homes, then curved into a street—narrower
and more exclusive—which two blocks later ended in a
T. Across from this intersection sat Ruth's yellow Honda
under a barbered maple, wheels turned out, the tail end
a foot into somebody else's driveway. There were no
spaces nearby. He parked around the corner and walked
back to Ruth's complex, hands in his pockets. The anxiety
had evaporated along with a pleasant anticipation he
hadn't noticed while it was there. What remained was
the leaden satisfaction of the inevitable taking its course.

From somewhere in the labyrinth of apartment ga-
rages, a child's voice cried, "Oly-oly, in free!"

The buzzer sounded as he approached the wrought-
iron gate and didn't cease until he was halfway up the
stairs. The door to her apartment was ajar, and he closed
it noiselessly behind him. Ruth's open kitchen faced him,
separated from the hallway by a breakfast bar and the
decorative skeleton of a wall; disordered ranks of utensils
and copper-bottomed pans hung from the frame. It was a
sight that never failed to irritate him, but Ruth loved the
openness of the design. The apartment was L-shaped.

The kitchen led naturally into a dining area in the corner, separate only by convention from the living room, which looked out onto the street. The bedroom and bath faced the kitchen on his left; their doors were closed.

"Lew."

She stood at the end of the spectral wall, her hands clasped at her waist, seeming even thinner with the light behind her.

"It's good to see you." In her soft, toneless voice was the hollow authority of a woman speaking through a microphone.

"Come in. Don't mind the mess," she said. "Would you like a drink?"

"Please."

The living room looked as though someone had set a fan in the middle of it and blown everything into random order along the walls. Sewing patterns drooped like pennants from the bookshelf; a half-finished blouse lay across the sewing machine; an art poster, still in its plastic, sat cockeyed in the overstuffed chair. There were letters splayed open on the desk amid torn envelopes, a stack of sheets, a stack of envelopes.

"I have white wine, beer. And bourbon. I have some bourbon."

"I'll take a beer," he said.

The mess was wrong, the closed doors were wrong, the presence of bourbon was wrong. A faint stale smell, the odor of mulch, hung in the room, and the asphalt taste was on his tongue again. He felt resigned, without knowing why. His thoughts remained aloof and eccentric, refusing to merge into an idea. He wanted to sit but knew that if he did, he would begin to understand, so he walked instead toward a splotch of yellow light on the living room floor, straight into it as if it might lift him into the afternoon sun.

"Lew?"

Her voice drew him back. To cover his retreat, he righted the print on the chair, a Renoir: a girl wearing a blue hat sitting in a theater box, a bouquet of wildflowers clutched in both hands.

Ruth came up beside him. "*La Première Sortie.* Do you like it?" She handed him a bottle and a glass.

"I like the line." He pointed to the diagonal curve of the theater box. "I wish there were more of her."

Ruth laughed. "So does she, probably. She's young."

She took him by the elbow and led him back to the dining area. "Come, I have something to tell you."

He resented her hand on his arm. Now there would be a story and excuses. A box would be opened. They'd put things inside, then close it and set it on a shelf, and that would be an understanding. The table was covered with crumbs. She was wearing a green silk blouse he'd given to her years ago and a red neckerchief knotted over the scar. Her hands were trembling.

"You've probably guessed already. I've got a guy." A melancholy smile accompanied her announcement, as if it were a joke and the joke was on her. "But that's not all. We're getting married next Sunday at the registry or at St. Mary's, depending on which side the priest's conscience lands."

Lew continued to stare at her hands, pleased that his attention could make them shake so violently. "What am I supposed to say?"

"How should I know? You might be disappointed or angry—or relieved, for that matter. You might congratulate me. You might ask who he is."

"Is that why I'm here?"

"Sweet Christ, Lew! After eight years, I thought you deserved an explanation."

The recipient of this solicitude grimaced as he twisted off the bottle cap and stared dumbly at the vapor that rose from the opening. Then he poured beer into the glass. It wasn't pain he felt, but an absence of will that ached like sunlight in the eyes. He wasn't unhappy, yet ironically he felt betrayed. But he could not imagine what he should have done or what he would have gained from it. The dull, unhurried throb in his ears measured the silence.

He tried to face her but couldn't. There were shadows, black near the window, almost transparent in the corner where the two of them sat; he scanned them, wishing he could be as diaphanous as the discoloration of the wall that rippled when he raised the beer to his lips. On the counter by the sink, behind a grease-gummed broiler rack, lay an empty bottle of champagne.

"You must be desperate," he said.

"No, I'm in love. Not everything happens according to plan."

"Three weeks."

"Two, really. The first one doesn't count. We were . . . what? Letting go, I guess. Don has just been through a divorce, and I've hardly been through anything."

"So you decided to do it quick, before you had time for second thoughts."

She shrugged, not dismissing the idea so much as denying its importance.

"And what if, three weeks from today, you decide that you've made a mistake?"

"Then we'll have made a mistake—a big, horrible, messy one. At least I'll have something exciting to regret."

Lew studied the streaks of light on his glass, annoyed by a sense that nothing he could say would hurt her. Above her head was a pendulum clock whose bob hung motionless.

"Your clock's stopped."

"Yes." Now it was Ruth's turn to grimace. She glanced over her shoulder at it. "Twelve o'clock exactly. Last

night we had a celebration, the two of us. I was tipsy and
Don was at least three drinks to the good of me. And we
were dancing, sort of, when the poor clock began to clang
out midnight—you know how awful it sounds. Well, Don
reached over and clobbered it. So, for the moment, anyway, I'm eternal."

The ache was gone, dissolved by the image of the two
of them, glued together, bumping through the house in a
drunken parody of dance. He thought: I'm alone. He
heard his footsteps echoing in the halls of the house on
Blackstone Street, clear and oddly comforting. Perhaps
because Ruth had looked over her shoulder, Lew remembered Evelyn Weiss in her red shirt calling, "Dulcy!"

"Sounds like he has a temper."

"Oh, stop pussyfooting! Of course he has a temper.
He's an emotional man—demanding, suspicious, tight
with money. Would you like me to go on? He pushes
himself too hard and drinks like a fish, and at least once
a day he makes me want to scream. So what? I need a
good scream."

He watched her hands explode into the air like startled
birds and undulate above the table with the clumsiness of
small children. Her gestures, as she spoke, stumbled over
each other, retreated, apologized, then rushed out to
stumble again.

"When I do scream, he screams back. I think he enjoys
it. Lord, I never thought I'd love a man who shouts at me.
I had my rules all laid out, everything in order. Then the
truth came along with a red nose and a smoker's cough,
and the whole kaleidoscope shifted. Look at me—shy
Ruth, meticulous Ruth. I wanted a man, I seduced him, I
made him love me, and look at this place. I can't keep
anything straight!"

Lew drifted further into his own meditation. This was
what he'd fought in her for eight years, this sentimental
romanticism. Every bit of bric-a-brac that caught her

fancy she imagined a work of art, every toad was a prince in disguise.

"I know there's a God—go ahead, grin! You and everybody else I know. But when you're happy, you begin to see connections. Look at me. I've had only two pills this week. No, I take that back—three. I took one before we talked to the priest. Isn't that miraculous, after four a day? Three weeks ago I walked into a pharmacy shaking so badly that when I tried to find my prescription I dumped my purse on the floor, and Don, bless him, came out from behind the counter and held me while I cried— didn't try to console me at all—and gave me a free box of Kleenex. He told me he knew exactly how I felt, that he'd felt the same way when Boston lost the World Series in 1967—teasing me. For maybe ten seconds I hated that man—imagine comparing my trauma to a baseball game! But he was laughing, which made me laugh, and before I could make myself angry again, I was in love. The pharmacy was happenstance, the purse was an accident, and Don intuitively said the right wrong thing. Don't tell me that wasn't Providence!"

Lew wasn't listening. He was thinking how little he'd lost, how much there was to be gained. Ruth would still be his friend; they could have their lunches and occasional outings, poking through antique shops. He rather preferred it that way. When he left he would call a number in Brookline, and a woman who knew his tastes would arrange to take care of the rest. Tonight he would have a woman prettier than Ruth, younger than Mrs. Weiss, and there would be no complications. He would take her out to dinner and then to a hotel, where she would slip out of her clothes, and do what he wanted, and he would never have to worry how she felt about it.

"I'm sorry. I shouldn't have gone on like that." Ruth took a sip of his beer.

Lew could not be sure of what she meant but felt encouraged that she was apologizing. It might have been the afterglow of his reverie, but that simple gesture—reaching across the table, drinking, replacing his glass—seemed quite alluring and mysterious. She'd thrown herself at the mercy of an emotion, she could drink from his glass.

"I'm not trying to gloat. Believe me."

"We're still friends," he agreed. "We'll see each other now and then."

"How?"

The question echoed in the room as if it had just been stripped of its furnishings.

"Lunch. Maybe an afternoon at the markets."

"Lew. No." She would not meet his eyes.

"He can't be that jealous."

She rocked as she spoke, arms crossed. "He has nothing to do with it. . . . Oh, damn."

When she glanced up, Lew saw, briefly, two yellow feet on a white bedspread and heard his mother spitting into the toilet.

"Lew, I'm sorry. Truly I am. Please try to understand. I don't want to be your friend. I don't want anything to do with who I used to be: with you or the job or this apartment. That's over. Don and I are very different people. Our marriage could last a week or a lifetime, but the change is permanent. You . . . I don't know how to put this nicely. You'd be underfoot."

The ache returned to his eyes and jaw, and he could feel the tiny explosions in his belly that were forcing him to breathe. Each burst of sensation was distinct and unbelievable. He could only respond, "Don't be silly."

Ruth did not answer.

"We've been friends for years. There are things that die without someone to remember them with."

"Good. Let them die."

"Ruth!" An angry pain knotted in his temples. "Talk to Don—he'll agree with me. You can't cut off your past."

She squinted at him askance, one brow raised, then pushed back her chair from the table. "All right. But don't expect anything."

Martin Cavanaugh spit out a piece of gristle and pointed to the television on the kitchen counter. "It's six, Mary. You want to turn on the news?"

"You've got hands," his wife retorted, and scooped out a second helping of chicken and rice.

Four childish voices, clamoring unintelligibly, subsided enough for one to be heard above the others. "And he made Kevin cry," it declared, implying that the act should carry the same penalty for neighbors as it did for brothers.

"It doesn't surprise me," his father allowed. "What I want to know is why Kevin, eh? Why not one of you?"

"You said we had to let him play with us." This came from the eldest in a tone of wounded self-righteousness.

"Don't give me that shit!" Spoons clacked against Corelle plates. Four anxious faces froze into attitudes of watchful innocence. "You sent him down there to get dumped on. Is that your idea of play?"

The children exchanged coded glances. Mrs. Cavanaugh smiled.

"Who kicked it down there, anyway? I know it wasn't Kevin."

Three faces turned toward one, and the one shouted angrily back at them. "It wasn't me, it was Dulcy!"

Martin Cavanaugh frowned. "Who the hell is Dulcy?"

"She's *your* daughter."

Evelyn Weiss lifted the martini her husband had proffered by its stem—twelve parts Dutch gin, one part Italian vermouth, with an olive.

"Two hours she was gone. You should have seen her,

bloody knees and scratches all over. And all she had to say for herself was, 'I lost the time, Mama.' Lost the time!"

His wife's vehemence brought a surge of desire, which Alex Weiss hid beneath a sympathetic cough. "How did she get the scratches?"

"I don't know. They were playing some game, and one of the kids pushed her into a bush—or so she says."

Thoughtfully, he pinched the flesh beneath his chin, shook it, and smiled. The idea of his daughter as a gladiator appealed to him. His arms ached from the gutters, but appraising his wife's upturned face, he wondered what she would say if he carried her to the couch.

"I'm not sure we should punish her."

"What punishment? A roomful of toys and a TV? I made her take a bath; that's the closest she came to punishment."

Bowing over her, rather formally, he kissed her on the temple, on the cheek, and as she lifted them to him, lightly on the lips.

Evelyn Weiss studied her husband. "You know what I think?"

"What?"

"I think I'd better set this drink down before we spill it."

Ruth, feeling the floor beneath her feet again, laughed up to the man who'd just kissed her, a laugh he did not like.

"He wants me to talk it over with you and call him later. Isn't that ludicrous?"

Don didn't think it was ludicrous, but he didn't say so. His tongue scraped dryly along the inside of his cheek, reminding him that he wanted a drink. "What am I supposed to do?"

"Not a thing."

"Are you going to call him?"

"No. Let him rot. Teach him what it feels like."

Turning his back, Don rummaged among the newly washed dishes for an old-fashioned glass. "You want a drink?"

"No, thank you."

He found one, set it in a niche in the refrigerator door and pressed the button for chopped ice. "Ho, boy!" he said. "Remind me not to get on your bad side."

Ruth laughed once more, this time less vengefully. "Don't worry. I will."

A slim black-haired girl wandered into the bar of the Miramar Hotel, glanced at her watch, and blinked into the gloom. Heads turned. She wore a bright flower-print silk shift and sandals and looked like a coed dressed to meet her father. Her arms were bare, her eyes deep-set and fixed in a quizzical expression as if she'd just heard something odd and was waiting for someone to make sense of it. Quietly she set her purse on the bar and waited for the bartender to notice her. The purse was too large, a squarish lump of black suede made uglier by a number of bulging, zippered pockets. When the bartender broke away from the men he'd been arguing with, he grinned at her and pointed across the bar. Several eyes followed her as she approached a booth in the corner.

"Lew?" she asked. Her voice carried no farther than a whisper.

The man in the booth nodded.

"I'm Valerie. May I?"

"Of course."

She slid in across from him, pushing her purse ahead of her, and tugged at her skirt, glancing curiously around the room. She stretched demurely and smiled. "I . . . Teresa couldn't make it, but she and I are close friends, and she didn't want you getting lonely. Do you mind?"

"No." He thought of the woman on the phone admonishing him to call earlier. "Did she . . . ? "

"Don't worry. She told me all about you—it made me a little envious, you know? I've always been attracted to mature men. They know what they want, and they're not afraid to take charge."

"Would you like a drink?"

She shook her head apologetically. "I'm underage."

Lew felt a sharp pang of pleasure. She seemed quite sophisticated for her age, and the dress, despite its simplicity, looked expensive. "I thought we might go to Pier Four if you like."

She smiled. "That's sweet! My father took me there a couple of years ago when he was in town." Her leg brushed his briefly under the table. "We're going to have fun."

The words thickened on his tongue. "I'd like to play a game."

"What sort of game?" There was an edge to her voice.

Lew's hands were clasped loosely on the table in front of him, one thumb caressing the other. "Tonight," he explained, "I don't want you to be Valerie. I want you to be someone else."

"No problem. I'm a good actress." Reaching across the table, she rested her fingertips on his wrist. Her voice deepened. "But you've got to help. You're the director. You have to tell me who I am."

Naomi didn't remember to eat until she had negotiated a place on the living room sofa, pressing aside the loose spring that wandered beneath the cushions like the ghost of Hamlet's father, and then it was too late. She didn't feel hungry anyway, never felt hungry anymore. From a glass-windowed case in the parlor, she'd taken a book at random, avoiding those volumes she and the women of her sodality had forced themselves to wade through—Gibbon's *Decline,* Lamb's *Essays*—which were displayed in their dust jackets on the wraparound shelves in the piano corner. The ones inside the locked case were romances she'd carried like a hope chest into her marriage, had loaned to her children, read and reread for over sixty years: Joseph Lincoln and Jeffrey Farnol and the man she always referred to as Winston Churchill–the–writer to distinguish him from the obscene little man with the cigar. These were books she loved as she once thought you loved a man, without judgment, requirement, or hesitation.

The gold print on the spine had worn away, and the shadow it left was too dim for her eyes. It fell open to the title page, the cracked spine revealing a flimsy grid of cloth.

A PAGEANT OF VICTORY
by Jeffrey Farnol

She remembered at once, a girl with Indian blood or stolen by Indians, something like that. A good deal of sneaking past outposts in canoes. Married a fool and thought herself happy because she'd escaped a bigger fool.

Now she would need the magnifying glass, but it wasn't on the end table or the sofa beside her. Out of habit, she paused to confirm her privacy, glaring into the black mouth of the fireplace, then picked up the book and found the magnifying glass in her lap.

"Shit!"

She held it just above the page, and the words surfaced as if they had risen from the bottom of a pond.

Blodwen stood where she might watch the road and the river, this river of her dreams, flowing down towards her from the wonders of the North to lose itself in the deep, leafy solitudes of the vast wilderness.

Naomi's stomach was growling, but she still felt no hunger, only a strange vertigo as if the words were making her dizzy.

Before her the road and the river, leading to a world of vivid life and action, behind her my lord George Charteris' great House of Wrybourne, throned upon its three terraces, builded sixty odd years ago by my lord's noble sire and like as possible to his ancestral home in England; a stately house beyond which clustered the thatched cottages and huts of his retainers and negro slaves.

But it was toward the road and silent river that Blodwen's long-lashed, sombre eyes were turned in dreamy contemplation until, startled by a faint sound, she turned with the lithe quickness of some shy forest creature and thus beheld the Earl's son, my lord Charles, and his companion, the young Marquis de Vaucelles.

And both young gentlemen were gazing at her and in the eyes of both she read that which deepened the bloom in her cheek and set her full-lipped mouth to sudden bitterness.

In the leather chair beside the fireplace, the *Herald* stretched across his lap like the blueprints of some vast estate, her husband sat in his suit and collar on a Saturday, reading with his finger like a farmer. Howard was a decent man. An honest and dutiful man. A man who loved his children and never questioned how she spent his money. But she hated him, hated him so violently, she could barely sit in the same room with him without trembling. He expected so much without even realizing it because the things he wanted seemed so small to him: his

house must be properly kept, and the children well be-
haved, his meals on time, his shirts lightly starched, his
wife accommodating—all for a grown man who'd spent
his life pretending there was something mystical about
being a bricklayer. He hardly ever spoke to her or
touched her. All he ever gave her was money and expectations.

"My Lord," said she in her soft rich voice, "I am no
man's sport . . . take warning." The Marquis laughed, and
before she might prevent, had set arm about her slender
waist; but with a supple ease she broke his hold and threw
him off so strongly that he staggered.

"Mordieu!" he exclaimed, straightening hat and wig,
"but this is appetizing! She is to tame and gentle, this one!
Regard now and I—"

"No, no," said Charles interposing, "let be, Gaspard,
she's a sullen baggage; 'stead o' being grateful for a gentle-
manly proffer she's apt to flash steel."

"Say'st thou, my dear Charles?"

"Ay faith, she's done it ere now. Cut young Wimperis in
the arm scarce a month ago. Damme! You'd think her the
proudest fine madam of 'em all, must be sued and wooed,
'stead of a mere . . . "

"What, sir?" she demanded, as he hesitated. "Oh, pray
what . . . what am I?"

The glass slid down the page and lodged in the crevice
between the cushion and the arm of the sofa; the book
dropped to the floor. She saw them go, but they seemed
to be too far away to intervene. A sudden clamor of clocks
striking the half hour woke her to the fear of strangers in
the room; but the fear subsided with the chimes, and she
fell quickly into the dreamless daze that was all she had
left of sleep.

•   •   •

The room stank of smoke. Valerie pushed the phone and the reading lamp against the wall to make a place for her purse. There were the usual furnishings—a bed, two low-backed overstuffed chairs, a desk/bureau, a nightstand. The walls, inevitably, were beige, the wood blond, the upholstery and spread interwoven with orange and rust. A collage of beige, orange, and rust papers, decoratively torn, hung over the headboard.

She unzipped the purse and removed a small lavender travel pouch. "I have to go to the bathroom."

Lew draped his coat over the television and sank into a chair. Over dinner, the girl had got him talking about Oriental rugs, her foot playing under the cuff of his trousers, until his voice had gone hoarse and his food was too cold to eat. He wondered if she could afford such things or if she was just humoring him, tediously.

Underwater voices came to him from the other side of the wall. The toilet flushed, but the girl did not come out. He tried to imagine what she might be doing but could not. A vague terror gripped him, and for a moment, he saw the freeway and the truck ahead of him, felt himself sucked under its wheels.

"Ready when you are." She smiled.

The hotel light had washed the delicacy from her features. She appeared pale and dull, and her shift hung loosely from her breasts, reminding him of the dresses worn by poor farm women in Depression-era photos. For a moment, she was dull, venal, prematurely old, and the vision excited him in a way that her youth and sensuality had not.

He loosened his tie. "Did you bring . . . ? "

"Sure." She rummaged through her purse and removed a suede whip, rolled tight, with a handle like a golf club's. On the bed, it uncoiled like a spring. "Be gentle. I haven't done this before."

"Good." He unfolded himself from the chair and hung

the tie, still looped, around the TV's vestigial antenna.
"You needn't act, just do as I say.

"You are a servant girl in a country village, one of the
many children of a curate. Your stepmother sent you into
day service when you were ten and whipped you with a
belt if your employer complained. When you were fifteen,
the steward of the squire's estate brought you to the
manor house. The housekeeper gave you a dress and
taught you to fix your hair. From her, you learned to clean
the silver and crystal and to serve at table. Sometimes
you slept in her bed, and she touched you in places you
had never been touched before.

"To you, a poor girl, the house was like a cathedral,
with its high ceilings and its tapestries and its dark oak
wainscoting. You felt rich and safe. You wanted to stay
there forever."

Valerie sat on the bed with her hands in her lap like a
child, blinking at the wall. He reached around her, letting
his hand brush her breasts. He hefted the whip. It was
light, soft leather.

"The master is a bachelor, a shy man with few friends,
a collector of antiques and wine. There were rumors of
perverse pleasures, of young girls ruined, but you dis-
counted them because he was quiet and spoke gently.

"Open the drapes." She obeyed with a shrug, her body
surfacing and receding beneath the dress as she tugged
at the cord. Then she turned and, with a little grin, curt-
seyed.

"After a while, you realized that you had caught the
master's eye. He would watch you at your duties. When
he spoke, he'd touch your arm. Soon (it all seemed very
natural), you were the one who served him when he took
tea alone, you were the one who brought him his pipe
when he smoked in the garden, you were the one who
tidied his bedchamber. When he discovered you reading
a novel, he gave you the run of his library."

Outside the room, rain had begun to fall. The flow of lights from the street played faintly against dark, glass-fronted skyscrapers. Directly across from them was an office building checkered with lighted windows. Lew liked the idea that someone across the way might see him with this girl.

"You were not naive. You knew what he was leading up to, but you also had your fantasies. You polished the silver and the crystal. You dusted the portraits of fine ladies in beautiful dresses, and you dreamed of occupying the empty seat at the mistress's end of the oak dining table. Take off your clothes.

"Slowly. One day, as you were undressing in your tiny upstairs room, the door opened. The master, still in his riding clothes, pressed his hands over your mouth and flung you down on your bed, and took your maidenhood. When he was finished with you he left without a word and you wept, thinking you had lost everything."

Her breasts were small, the nipples pink. She let her panties fall to her ankles, then kicked out one leg, holding them up to him with her toes. "Next time I'll wear more clothes."

"Hush." They were perfumed, and his chest tightened as he breathed their scent. "After that, you came to his room whenever he asked, and he locked the door behind you. He told you what to do, and you obeyed, no matter how cold or cruel his demand. You were miserable, but afraid to do anything else. He was a powerful man, and you had nowhere to go."

With the handle of the whip, he probed the lips of her vagina, felt the cold breath of his fear returning. "Lie down on the bed and turn your face toward the window."

Quickly, awkwardly, Lew pulled off his clothes and stood next to the bed. He drew the strap over her body, hardening as she moved under its touch.

"In time, you became as depraved as he was. You looked forward to your debasement. You anticipated his

demands and obeyed before he could even form the
words. Every night you sank a little deeper. He told you
the obscenities of his heart, and you acted them out. You
demanded clothes, jewelry, money, and occasionally he
gave them. The other servants were wary of you, afraid
of your power over him. But still you polished the silver."

Behind the locked windows of his mother's dining
room breakfront, tiers of Gorham crystal glistened like a
waterfall. The whip descended. There was a small sound
like a child's clap, the girl hissed, and across the little
walrus smile at the base of her buttocks, a faint pink
stripe appeared. His penis throbbed but did not rise. He
worked quietly, methodically. More stripes—across her
legs, her buttocks, her back—crisscrossing in strange patterns like the tissue of a scar. The tightness in his chest
began to ease, as if something in him had cracked and a
great reservoir of darkness were draining out, so that
when he paused for breath he felt almost nerveless, except for the ache in his groin.

The first marks had faded. He ran his fingers gently
over the ones that remained. "He beat you and called you
whore, but you didn't mind. His beatings were never as
bad as your mother's." He slipped them down among the
dark hairs that fringed the crease of her buttocks, along
the smooth skin of her inner thigh—and pinched until
she cried out in pain. His penis remained at half-staff like
a wilted flag. "You noticed that he no longer traveled to
London, that he was seldom away overnight and seldom
invited guests for the weekend, that he was impatient
with any duty that kept him away at night." Between the
towers of the city gray clouds hung like Spanish moss,
tinted a sickly pink by the lights below.

"Get up and go to the window." She rolled from the
bed, lithe and easy, and stood with her back to him, staring out at the building across the street. "Turn around
and kneel."

Between their neighbor and the scythe of lights that

bordered the harbor, the city huddled in the murk like a graveyard of ships on the bottom of the ocean. "You knew that the deeper you went, the more he'd depend on you, that someday the two of you would fall so far, he would never be able to let you go."

Aid and Comfort

HE would have had the world in his eyes. The day was clear and smogless. From the top of the ridge, the boy could have seen across San Francisco Bay and the Alameda all the way to Mt. Diablo, the water a smoky jade, the mountains dim and blue in the distance. Then the long plunge down Clipper Street, with the sheer rock of Diamond Heights on one side and a few apartment buildings clinging to the other. Gradually the view would have slipped away—first the city, then the bay and the mountains—and from that point on, my powers of imagination are no good to me. What happens to the solid world when a person loses control of it? Does it fly apart or does it freeze into a single terrifying vision?

After the bay disappears, a small park replaces the rock. The road narrows from four lanes to two. Parked cars line the curb, and stucco cottages crowd the walk, perched on cement-walled terraces that give the effect of a giant stairstep descending. Near the foot of the hill, the houses back away from the street, gain a story, and put on multicolored Victorian facades. "Carnival houses," my ex-husband calls them, embarrassed by so many colors. In one of them, my daughter and I live.

This has always been a good area to raise a child—clean, fairly quiet, conservative by San Francisco standards, out of the way, with quite a few single women like myself. There are few crimes, but lots of accidents.

We've gotten used to the accidents; that is, as a neighborhood we've come to have habits and expectations about them, like people who are used to floods. Most drivers panic when their brakes go, which is probably why few people have been injured and only one, since we've lived here, has died. They pump the brakes a few times, feel the momentum building, and steer into the closest stationary object. Quite a healthy reaction, that.

When we hear the crash, we rush out with our first-aid

kits and fire extinguishers, our flares, crowbars, garden
hoses, flashlights, chocks, traffic cones, blankets, coffee—
whatever we've found over the years might come in
handy—and descend upon the victims en masse. It's an-
archy, pure and simple, and often comical, like the time
we argued about moving an injured man while his car
rolled down the hill and into a laundromat. But we know
what we are doing. By the time the authorities arrive—
fire truck, patrol car, ambulance, always in that order—
the fires are out, traffic has been diverted, and the victims
sit huddled in blankets, drinking coffee.

You come to count on this after a while. You contrive a
dream of miraculous balance. You hear screams of pain,
you see cars on fire, and you feel no fear because you
don't expect anyone to die.

I remember the boy as he sat beside me, straight and
pale and alone, as foolish and stubborn in his remorse as
he had been in his attempt to steer out of trouble when
the brakes went, and there was a distance between us far
greater than the one between my house and the blue
mountains across the bay. Never have I felt so sorry for
someone, and never has sympathy seemed more futile.

The day before the accident, when I left to take my
daughter to St. Paul's, the surveyors had just set out their
signs at the top of the block. A crew of three were unload-
ing their gear from the back of an orange pickup. By the
end of the afternoon they had worked halfway down,
speckling the road with those dabs of hot pink that pre-
sage the arrival of jackhammers. The next morning they
were parked in front of me, their orange vests on my
hood and a transit propped against the driver's-side door.
They took their time removing them, too. One (I recall
sandy hair and a beard) asked my daughter, Jill, something about becoming a nun.

"How does his wife stand it?" she fussed when we were
in the car.

"His wife?"

"That beard! God, it makes me itch just thinking about it."

My daughter is twelve, and her complaints often sound like confessions. "Maybe he's not married," I said.

"No wonder."

Later, as we wended through the droves of blue-and-green tartans in front of the school, she added, "I hate this uniform."

The rest of the morning was spent sanding down the small drawers of a turn-of-the-century American secretary desk one of my ex-husband's law partners had bought for his house. I began restoring furniture some years ago when we separated, and after the divorce it became a profession. A rather monkish profession, perhaps, and not entirely satisfying—aesthetically or financially—for I have found there is less beauty in what people try to save than superstition and vanity. My ex sends a lot of business my way. Not out of love, I suspect, but so I will listen to his interminable, lonely telephone calls whenever some twenty-year-old snow bunny drops him for the trainer at her health club.

After lunch, I abandoned the secretary for the splintered leg of an ugly but very old pine blanket box, which probably should have been chopped into kindling a century ago. There was no saving the original, so I cut a new piece of wood and drilled holes. The owner would complain. They always do. Owners of antiques are great believers in miracles. I'd already set the dowels and drilled the new leg when a truck's horn and the concussions of an accident broke my concentration. Then *boom!* The whole house shook with the impact. I threw a jacket over my work clothes, but there was that damned leg with the glue getting tacky, and I knew the piece could be ruined if I had to drill it again. So I quickly set the leg and wiped it clean and vised it to the stump with a C clamp before I ran outside.

I'm not sure what I expected to find, certainly not what

I saw. Wedged into the gap where the steps breached our terrace, a huge rust-eaten dump truck filled with gravel hung over the terrace wall as if its enormous grille were browsing the ice-plant border. I leaned against a porch pillar. It looked absurd, almost innocent in its enormity, but it made me shiver all the same. The mayhem was spectacular. Down the hill, four parked cars had been flung out in a zigzag toward the median. On my uphill neighbor's sidewalk a van lay on its side, the hood sprung, the engine partly disemboweled. At the intersection a car had been crushed, and farther up the street were some fender-benders caused by startled drivers veering out of the way. Splashes of glass and gasoline were everywhere.

A crowd had already gathered around the truck, so I climbed through the terraced yards to where I thought my help might be needed most—the car at the intersection. Its rear end had been ripped away, and the hatch-back door and part of the roof curled over the pavement like a wave about to break. Nancy from across the street had opened the driver's door and appeared to be talking to someone inside. One person, at least, was conscious. Somewhere behind me, a fire truck revved its siren.

Scraps of metal and tiny fragments of glass were strewn over the pavement. The car's rear bumper lay in the near gutter atop a warning sign that the surveyors had placed at the crossroads. Its backseat lunged halfway out of the hole where the hatch had been. The driver was sitting up, holding on to the steering wheel. There was blood on her face, but she was directing one of the young men who lived in the house on the corner as he chased after her belongings. I gathered a few glossy brochures from the pavement whose covers depicted a woman typing a multicolored graph into a computer.

The victim dismissed them with a wave—"I've got bushels of those." Unsteadily, she pulled herself out of the car and to her feet.

The young man's housemate loped by crying, "I'll bring them around!" "Them" being the fire truck picking its way through the traffic below.

"Invoices," the driver of the car moaned, wincing as she touched the ribs on her left side. "Three sheets of paper—white, yellow, and pink."

A woman I didn't recognize strolled down to join us. I smiled at her, but she didn't smile back. It was a weird search. No one smiled or talked. They just roamed about with their eyes to the ground, cocooned in themselves. I asked Nancy, "What's up?" But she pretended not to hear.

Below, the fire truck blasted its horn, trying to turn onto Castro Street through a small mob of kids from the junior high playground at the bottom of the hill.

"Look!" The victim kicked at a wheelless axle that stuck out from under her car like the tail of a Q. "How close can you get?"

"But you're all right," I said, trying to soothe her. I've learned you have to be a bit firm or they'll talk themselves into hysteria.

A ragged burst of laughter sent her reeling against the torn metal, but she didn't seem to feel it. "Look! One foot, two feet . . . "

"Calm down."

"I could have been hamburger!" she shrieked, then buckled at the knees as if she were about to faint.

The man from the corner dropped the papers he'd gathered and caught her arm, and Nancy helped him ease her toward his terrace wall. When I followed, Nancy waved me away. "Leave her alone."

For a moment, I just stood there in the middle of the road, watching a woman I did not know gingerly lift a slip of pink paper from a puddle of gas. A patrol car nosed in behind the wreck, and I could hear the fire truck rumbling up Diamond. Several boys from the junior high darted past in a skein. I grabbed one and shouted, "Get back where you belong!" And he obeyed, surprisingly. They all did. I must have sounded dangerous.

I followed them down, still fuming. A second patrol car had blocked the road at Castro, and the mob of kids, shying back from it, revealed a broken tripod lying across the grate of the storm drain. That meant nothing to me. The woman at the intersection had not died, so somehow, to my mind, no one had.

On the terrace wall across from our house I noticed a young man, hands laced in his lap, his longish black hair stark against his white T-shirt. He stared wide-eyed at the truck as if it were a screen. He was alone. I thought, idiots!

At my approach his eyes dropped, and he began to dig at the grass in a sidewalk crack with his toe. Before I could ask, he answered my question, "Yeah, I'm the one."

"So am I. That's my house you nearly remodeled."

He blinked as if someone had shone a flashlight in his eyes.

I was reminded of Jill when she was small, perched on the edge of the bed after I'd wakened her, gazing in a stupor at the wall. Touch her, and she'd cry out in pain.

I sat next to him. "Here, let me loan you my jacket."

"I'm okay." My face might have been the reflection on a window he was looking through.

"You're in shock." I took his hand. "Feel the difference?" His fingers were freezing, and mine, to my embarrassment, were still tacky from glue.

He shrugged.

"Don't take it so hard," I said. "This happens all the time."

"Not to me."

And in the anguished focus of his gaze I knew, even before I followed it into the shadows beneath the truck, what I would find. The body lay on its back, one knee crooked, arms flung to either side of a set of double wheels, the head invisible under the tires. It wore boots and jeans and an orange protective vest.

"Oh, God!"

I tore at the glue on my palm, and it came off in shreds like dried skin. My words returned to me, and my body burned with shame. The temptation was to apologize, to beg his forgiveness, but luckily I had the sense to keep my mouth shut. He didn't need any more words.

About the dead man there was the placidness of the irrevocable, an awful sort of calm that was almost beautiful. Someone I had seen, perhaps spoken to that morning, had been crushed to death, but I could not feel his loss, only a powerless sense of guilt.

Oblivious to me, the boy contemplated what he had done. What he needed now, absolutely, I thought, was not to be alone. A dark runnel of water foamed down the gutter. The firemen were hosing down the road above.

The promenade had begun: schoolchildren, shoppers from Twenty-fourth Street, mothers with small children from the park, old folks from apartments in the valley. They spread and gathered like shoals of fish, gravitating toward us as they passed the truck, nervous as tourists passing the curtained door of a sex club, with a quick dip now and then as one of them peeked under. From where we sat, all we saw were their backs and the sides of their faces.

An ambulance arrived, then another, lights flashing. A police sergeant materialized from the crowd and pointed his clipboard at us.

"Don't go anywhere," he said.

A man who lives two houses down from me stopped by to say he'd called the number on the door of the dump truck.

The boy acknowledged him with a faint smile.

Eventually, the passing crowd seemed to revive my

companion. His color returned, and he began to glance around. I asked if there were someone I could call for him. He rubbed the heel of one hand against his jeans as if he were planing the leg smooth and said, "I should've run it off the road up there."

The passersby obscured and revealed the body in the shadows. "You couldn't have known."

"Hell, I couldn't."

Occasionally, a neighbor hurried by on the usual errands. A few, mostly men, loitered near the truck. A patrolman maneuvered a stick with a small wheel at one end from the body to a spot the sergeant was marking with his foot. I tried to imagine their report: a neat, uncomplicated story illustrated with numbers and diagrams.

"Maybe if there was more time," the boy continued. "But I kept trying things, you know? I put the emergency on and figured I could engine-brake down in low. Didn't think about the load. And when the gears stripped, there was nothing but that sign in the road. Looked like all I needed to do was hold on. Then that car pulled out in front of me, and this guy—I don't know where he came from."

Not a soul between his truck and the flat stretch at the bottom. "I might have done the same thing," I said.

I wouldn't have, of course. With the junior high below and Church Street and its trolley line not far beyond, there was the possibility of a massacre. But I could see how the road must have appeared to him in that instant after the gears had failed—steep and narrow, but unaccountably clear—and I could understand the temptation to believe in miracles.

The police crossed toward us, the sergeant with his clipboard under one arm and the patrolman tapping his stick on the road like a blind man. Badges and guns and blue shirts—with the boy's vision of the scene still intact, I felt as if they were speaking directly to my nerves.

"You're guilty," they whispered. "There are no excuses."

"Watch it," I warned the boy.

The sergeant scowled. "Watch what? We just need
some questions answered, son. After that, you ought to
go with the ambulance, let the doctors check you out. The
insurance companies . . . "

"Screw the insurance companies," the boy said.

"Up to you. Would you mind stepping over here?"

This was my cue to leap to my feet and ask, "Am I in
the way?" But I'd built up too much inertia to respond to
hints. If they wanted me to leave, they'd have to tell me.

The boy rose, brushing off the seat of his pants, and
ambled away with them, the patrolman's hand on his
shoulder. Only the cadence of their voices reached me,
the sergeant's quick and crisp, the boy's halting.

The crowd had thinned, and wreckers were removing
the damage above. I watched a third officer putter deter-
minedly around the truck. He squatted with his hand on
the huge gas tank behind the cab, crawled under to where
the universal hung obscenely like the genitals of some
monstrous male animal, then backed out and slipped into
the crevice between the bin and the wall. Above him, the
row of multicolored houses shone cheerily in the afternoon sunlight. Ours had been painted the month before
—a sandy brown, trimmed in azure and ultramarine—
much to the irritation of Jill's father, who believes that
paying the mortgage gives him the right to be consulted
every time I hammer a nail into the wall. Juxtaposed with
the truck, the house did look rather silly, a Victorian girl
in a bright frock confronted by a tank. But I liked the
silliness. It was sane and happy and vulnerable.

Nancy stopped, though I think she would have passed
without a word if I hadn't spoken her name.

"How is she?"

"Who knows? She calmed down a little before the ambulance took her away."

Two boys with a boom box strode past the truck in a chin-jutted pantomime of unconcern, measuring themselves by it.

"Does anyone know what happened?" I asked. "Those men must have had time to get out of the way."

"He didn't tell you?"

"I don't think he knows."

At the crosswalk one of the boys ran his hand, or something in his hand, across the hood of the patrol car, and they vanished around the corner.

"It was those damned sticks." She tried to shove her hands into her pockets, then realized her jeans were too tight. Neither of us smiled. "He went back for the sticks."

"You saw it?"

"Some. Either his foot slipped or he realized he couldn't make it. Anyway, he stopped. It looked as though the driver expected him to go on and tried to cut in behind."

The surveyor must have flown from the grille like a crumpled bird and then disappeared beneath the wheels. A mistake, certainly nobody's fault, but the driver would never believe that. He'd swerved right into a man.

All the shame and anger I'd felt when I'd first seen the body surfaced again, but I no longer knew what I was ashamed of or with whom I was angry.

"They let him sit here alone like a leper," I complained.

"What could they do?"

Sit with him, I thought, let him know he's still part of the human race. But I said nothing. Apparently, with tragedy, one takes sides. Nancy and I faced each other across the distance of our choices, and in that silence the cadence of voices ceased.

The patrolman climbed toward the truck while the sergeant remained astraddle the median taking notes. The boy sauntered back and plumped down beside me, and to my own amazement, I blushed. I hadn't realized until

then how much I doubted the comfort of my companion-
ship. Yet, as he leaned, elbows to knees, head in hands,
toward the body under the truck and fixed it with that
same blank, suffering gaze, I wished to God he had let
one of the ambulances take him.

"What did the police say?"

"Nothing. They're not going to arrest me, anyway."

The moment my attention was diverted, Nancy left. I
watched her weave through the zigzag of battered cars
and hated her with a disturbing intensity.

"Then you're free," I said to the boy.

He massaged his right eye. It was bloodshot and beginning to swell.

"It's not your fault," I added.

"Bullshit!" He smashed his fist against the terrace wall
so hard, I was surprised he didn't break his fingers. "The
man's dead! If I'd ditched it up there, he's alive."

People nearby turned to look. Seeing them, he ducked
and flexed his hand. "Sorry."

"That's all right."

I began to understand. For him, the facts reduced to a
simple drama—him, the truck, the victim. And a simple
fact—he had killed a man. There could be no extenuating
circumstances. The faulty brakes mattered as little, to
him, as the source of a fire would to a woman whose child
had died because she couldn't brave the flames. It was a
very old ethic for one so young—fate, retribution, courage, horror. He wanted to suffer, but he didn't know how.

Once the police had finished, the bureaucrats of death
made their appearance: the fire captain, a reporter, several insurance agents, and a fat, blue-uniformed fellow
with a kepi on his head and a huge badge the color of a
bronzed shoe on his chest, who introduced himself as the
deputy coroner. They performed their duties with defer-
ential assurance, paring the accident to fit into the spaces
on their forms and pocket notebooks. They stood apart,

just a bit, as if they were afraid the boy's pain might be infectious. He answered every question, signed beside every "X" in a round, awkward hand, never asking what any of it meant. I don't know which angered me more, the antisepsis of their attitude or the surrender in his. Lord, he would have confessed to murder if they had wanted it.

The boy was not without a certain craft, however. To the reporter and the insurance agents he gave a different name from the one he gave to the others. When we had a moment alone, he assured me that he wasn't lying. One was his mother's surname, the other belonged to his foster father; normally he went by the latter, but when he didn't want to be bothered, he gave the former, which was still his legal name. His mother didn't care; she lived in Florida.

Perhaps I should have warned him about giving out false information and so on, but his strategy pleased me. To have another name, another identity, to call upon whenever some ratty little creature demanded a piece of your flesh—what a privilege! Infantile, I admit, bought at the cost of whatever had made him a foster child and calculated to get him into more trouble than it saved him, but a privilege nonetheless.

I suggested that he phone his foster father, but he shrugged me off.

A car entered the blockaded area from above and parked in the downhill lane next to the overturned van. A thick, gray-suited man emerged and motioned to the sergeant. A police inspector, I thought. But then he slammed the door, and I saw that the name on the door was the same as the one in fading block letters on the door of the boy's truck. Instead of meeting the officer halfway, he leaned against his car holding his glasses several inches from his face and peering through them as if he'd just discovered they were dirty. The early part of their conversation was conducted with him muttering out of the side of his mouth to the sergeant as he cleaned his lenses. He didn't like the answers, apparently. Replacing his glasses, he interrogated the sergeant like a prosecutor, gesturing angrily in the direction of the truck with the white handkerchief still in his hand.

Meanwhile, an enormous wrecker crept downhill, its brakes squalling. Caught up in his rage, the newcomer was poking at the sergeant's chest with an index finger. The sergeant grabbed him by the wrist, while the wrecker maneuvered delicately around them and the truck and lumbered onto the sidewalk. I closed my eyes and breathed through the tightness in my chest. I remembered my ex-husband pacing the living room, with one hand in his back pocket and the other brandishing an index finger accusingly. That was his idea of a conversation, and not just with me—with his friends, his daughter, the people he met in stores. He couldn't even talk to himself without pointing.

When I opened my eyes again, the man in the gray suit was headed in our direction, limping a bit because his downhill foot kept slipping. He stopped before he reached the curb to pick up a small chunk of metal from the road and toss it into one of the yards.

The boy faced him silently.

"You fucking imbecile! Why didn't you come the long way around? Why didn't you at least put the damned truck in low?"

"It was in low."

"Sure." He was glaring up toward the top of the ridge, unable, I suspected, to meet his driver's eyes. "You're fired, Danny. And nobody around here's going to hire you, not even the cabs—I can promise you that. You've screwed me royally, and whether the cops do anything or not, I'm going to nail you to the wall, y'hear? As a favor to the fucking world!" There was a sob of genuine an-

guish in his voice. Again I was reminded, unpleasantly, of
my ex-husband—this time, lying in the snow at Squaw
Valley with his leg broken, screaming at the ski patrol, at
the paramedics, but mostly at me, as if he believed the
pain would go away once he'd blamed enough people for
it.

A man had climbed down from the big wrecker and
was guiding it back, a foot at a time, toward the bumper
of the truck.

"You said you knew this city," the owner cried. "You
said you could handle a rig. Look! That's a public em-
ployee. The city of San Francisco's going to roast me over
a slow fire. Twenty years down the shithole because of
you!"

The fist that Danny had made of his two hands tightened and released, and he frowned into the gap that
opened and closed between them.

"I should've run it off two blocks up, but I didn't have
the guts."

My heart sank. He wasn't defending himself, he was
just offering a proper target. His boss fell on it like a
hawk.

"Two blocks! You drove that thing without brakes for
two fucking blocks?"

The boy bowed his head, and the astonished owner
mouthed at me like a deaf person. In a slow crescendo he
began to rain down more and more abuse on that silent,
bent head. He was insane, stoned, a murderer, a faggot,
and there were several things that he was supposed to do
with his ass. The longer it went on, the more savage and
obscene it became. His accuser began to flail the air like
a man being swept away by a flood. The towing crew,
huddling with the police among our ice plant, turned to
watch. The passersby, the neighbors on their porch steps
listened from the comfort of their distances. No one
moved to help, not even me. I don't know why, except
that Danny did not protest.

Finally, and only out of sheer weariness, I interjected, "The brakes are yours."

"Keep your fat ass out of—"

I leapt up so fast, I nearly swooned into his arms. "Don't you 'fat ass' me, you bastard! One more word and I'll call that sergeant over here and file charges, don't think I won't!"

"What charges?" There was, beneath his flushed and contemptuous mask, a look that was almost grateful.

"Disorderly conduct, intimidation, perhaps assault. I'm sure the sergeant would be happy to help me find the appropriate words."

Two flabby fingers hung in midair about six inches from my nose, arrested by what vision I can't say.

"Every six months," he began, "those trucks—"

"Please. No more."

We stood together in uneasy silence until one of the wrecking crew called to him, and he went away, tying strings of adjectives to the word *bitch*.

I rubbed the backs of my thighs and savored the pull of gravity.

"What a hateful man," I said. "Why did you let him bully you?"

The boy frowned into the dark circle his hands had created. "He gave me a job."

From a squat the owner contemplated what lay beneath his truck, patting its side as if it were a racehorse gone lame.

I touched his shoulder. "Let me drive you home."

But he shook me off.

"It's over," I insisted.

The door of the wrecker slammed shut. One of the crew jumped onto the back. Two braided steel cables ran through a tall crane from the winch behind the cab. He released the hooks at the end of those cables, and the steel plate between them banged against the crane.

"You don't want to see this."

The eyes he lifted toward me were gentle and empty.
"Why would you?" I asked. "It won't help."

His answer was blotted out by the whine of the cables
descending. The sound—I don't suppose it was very loud
—gripped me like the scream of a child. I thought, no
more. If I could have thrown him over my shoulder and
carried him off, I might have done it, but I would not stay
for this. One of the men slid underneath the truck to
attach the hooks, and a gray hearse with the city seal on
its door eased into position nearby. A man in white took
a sheet-covered gurney from the back while his partner
unfolded a vinyl bag.

I fled. There's no other word for it, though I walked
away calmly enough. The keys were in the pocket of my
jacket, and my car was parked around the corner. I didn't
look back.

The inside of the car was like a furnace, and when I
shut the door, silence closed in on me. A number 24 bus
stood parked across the road. I watched the driver pull
down a sheet from his sun visor and make notes. The glue
had begun to peel off my fingers in tiny rolls. I rubbed
them against my jeans, but it wouldn't come off any
faster. The bus filled and departed. Only then did I turn
on the ignition and ease into traffic.

I circled the Mission District, with no idea of where I
was headed or why, slowing at every intersection, the
noise of the cables still vibrating within me. At each stop-
light someone would glance at me, it seemed, with a peculiar knowledge. A page of newspaper rolling in the
gutter, a flash of light from the hood of an approaching
car would throw me into a panic, and it would take all my
self-control not to swerve. I thought nothing, I imagined
nothing. The cars, the stores, the pedestrians flowed
across my windshield like reflections on the surface of a
deep river.

I began to talk to myself. Much of it was nonsense, and

a couple of times I caught myself rehashing old wounds
from my childhood. I tried to find the words to tell Jill
what had happened, but soon it seemed pointless. How
do you tell a twelve-year-old who believes that God holds
every one of us in His hands about the man whose brains
were ground into our cement? What good does it do to
call it an accident? The more I talked, the more incoher-
ent I became. When it came time to pick up Jill, I was
nearly hysterical.

Double-parked outside the school, I leaned on the
steering wheel with my head in my arms and tried to
pray, but the words staled in my mouth. I couldn't even
cry.

Suddenly, the street was awash with white blouses and
blue-and-green tartans. My daughter, her face distorted
by the curve of the window, was beating on the locked
passenger door.

She tossed her bookbag into the back and flung herself
into the car. "Jesus, what planet are you on?" She kissed
the cheek I offered, exposing two rows of stainless-steel
braces. "Did Dad call?"

Of all the questions she might have asked, that was the
one most likely to deflect me from the tragedy on the hill.
"No, why should he?"

"He said he'd talk to you."

"When did he say that?"

Instantly, as if a pair of sheers had been drawn in front
of her, she closed herself off.

"Jill, what is this about?"

"They're going skiing Friday, they want me to come
with them. Karen promised to teach me." All in a rush.

Karen was the latest in the series of lovers to whom my
husband had exposed Jill, and they were always very
sweet and young, and calculating, though I couldn't have
pointed that out to my daughter without starting a fight.
After her father and I had separated, I took a lover, and

my ex has never forgiven me. Under his influence, with some help from the nuns, Jill has begun to blame me, too.

"He gets you on Saturdays," I said.

"They're leaving Friday morning at nine."

"No." This was typical. "If he wants you, he can wait until school's out. If he doesn't . . . "

"That's not fair!"

Of course it wasn't fair, but some unfairnesses are truer than others.

With Jill settled against the door in accusatory silence, I found that I could report the accident without explanations. She didn't ask many questions—only if I'd seen it and if the victim had suffered. In case they were still at it when we returned, I reluctantly mentioned the crushed skull. She didn't respond, just folded a leg up against her body and rested her chin on her knee. A few blocks later she asked what I had against Karen.

"Do you have any money?" I countered.

My question evoked a sullen little grimace. "Eight dollars. Why?"

She'd had twenty yesterday morning. "When we get to the cleaner's, would you pick up your uniform? I forgot my purse."

"Forgot your purse!" she whooped. "With your driver's license and everything? You're falling apart. What if a cop pulls us over? Daddy would have to bail us out."

I prayed, Let them be gone. Let it be gone.

While my daughter ran into the shop, I drove around the block. The frustration returned. The boy was beside me, the boy with his infinite capacity for suffering and his bizarre sense of honor, and I could have screamed. How miserable he must have been, in his solitary world, waiting stoically as if he were expecting some message from the remains. Some things one should not be strong about.

She emerged and waltzed to the car, her uniform in its plastic sheath streaming behind her.

"You owe me six and a quarter. The one with the hennaed hair tried to stiff me out of a dollar, but I caught her."

"She makes mistakes the other way, too," I reminded her.

Jill appraised me quite openly. "How about if Daddy picks me up after lunch? I haven't got any real classes in the afternoon."

"Later!" It came out sharper than I had meant.

We drove in silence. The boy was still there, as tangible to me as if he were squeezed between us on the front seat. I thanked God I hadn't driven him home. As we turned onto Clipper, the hill loomed before us, chevroned in late afternoon shadows. Only the gaps where the cars had been revealed anything out of the ordinary. In the absence of what I had feared, a peculiar sense of loss spread through me like a chill, as though I'd come home and found the neighborhood razed.

Jill sighed noisily, then laughed at herself. "Was it gross?"

"No, but some things are worse for not being gross."

She folded her knee under her chin. "Yeah."

Children from the public school darted from the shadows or sauntered across the road with a nonchalance that reminded me of the boys with the boom box. They cast their bodies in front of the car like a challenge—change your course, slow down, wait. Arrogant brats, I thought. What a pleasure it would have been to ease my grille up to one of those sashaying rumps and give it a push. But the thought sickened me.

Now, as we neared the scene, Jill fired off one question after another. Why did the brakes fail? Where had the dead man been standing? How come our car wasn't hit? I answered shortly, annoyed by her excitement. Images of the wreckage returned to me, vague but powerful, the emotions a bit out of focus with their objects gone, yet clinging to me like the smell of smoke.

The road and sidewalk in front of our house were

stained where the firemen had hosed them down. Alone
on the playground, a child with a basketball bobbed and
weaved around imaginary opponents.

I parked behind a Jeep that the accident had missed.
Before I could get the wheels curbed, Jill had leapt out
and dashed across the road. I retrieved her uniform and
bookbag. The wall where the truck had lodged was crum-
bled, and the street glittered with tiny pieces of glass.
Balanced on top of the ruined wall, my daughter raised
her arms like a tightrope walker, the wind tossing her
skirt.

"Where was he?"

I thought: It might have been Daddy, love. It might have
been you. Leaning against the door, I felt a sudden spasm
of grief for the man who was nothing to her but a spot
where something terrible had happened. Ironically, the
surveyor's absence touched me far more deeply than his
dead body had. Whoever he was—his hopes, his dreams,
his pain—had been washed down a storm drain with a
fire hose because a simpleminded boy had trusted his
luck.

"Does it matter?" I asked.

She stumbled as she was jumping off but, accustomed
as she was to the grade, caught herself easily. In the anxious instant before she had found her feet, I saw, with
the same eyes that had seen the man's body fly from the
grille, a pale girl with long black hair reeling into the
road.

"Here?"

I didn't answer. She was standing right on top of it.

"You can't tell," she complained.

The metal skin of the door felt hot under my hand. A
man had died, and there wasn't even a mark. Nothing.
Then the shame I had carried like a fever broke into a
long, silent cry of outrage. The fool! The blind, stubborn
little shit! For him to see that sign, those men scattering,

the cars in the other lanes, and to believe he could make it! To believe that the laws of probability would miraculously suspend themselves as long as he could see his way clear! I hated him. I hated his ignorance, his cowardice, his miserable sense of honor. But most of all, I hated his suffering.

"Mom?"

Because it was dumb and blind and tomorrow would be just as dumb and just as blind, and there would be no helping him ever. I didn't care who was guilty or how much. I just wanted to pull him up by the hair and cry, "Damn you! Damn you to hell!"

"Mom, what's wrong?"

Strangely, though, at the height of this fury, I felt such a rush of tenderness that in the end I might have embraced him. Blinking back tears, I looked for my daughter, but the bright houses had melted, their colors running and mixing together, and for a moment I could not tell which one was mine.

Eagles

WHEN I got out of the Navy I didn't have a cent, didn't know anything except chasing shadows on a screen, and the only job I could find was as a bookkeeper in a tool and die shop in Seattle. The man asked me, "Do you have experience?" I said, "Sure." And he took my word for it. What I knew about bookkeeping could have fit on the head of a pin with room left over for the Lord's Prayer, but I figured out what the fellow before me had done and kept on doing it. After a while I wasn't a liar.

For thirty-odd years, that's the way it has been. I never ask myself if I'm qualified or if I know what the hell I'm doing. Those questions make you stop, and in this world, if you stop, somebody behind you is going to flatten your ass. I've taken what's come to hand and changed when the rules changed. The only question I've ever asked is, "Does it work?"

After a while, Winslow, the president of the company then, sent me to Tacoma to manage a shop he'd acquired. In three years I doubled their profits. How? Damned if I know. Later on, working out of the main office in Seattle, I midwifed a merger. What did I know about mergers? Nothing. Now I've got a door that says "President" and a secretary who won't let my best friend in without an appointment, and all I've ever done is ride the main chance and hold on. My fellow Rotarians see a railroad brakeman's son behind a big desk, and fairy tales light up their eyes. I'm a Horatio Alger hero, a man of vision and courage, living proof.

Shit. If I needed vision, I'd still be back in the shop. As my dad used to say, "Dreams don't make babies," and with twelve kids he should have known. During the War, I monitored radar on an aircraft carrier and dreamed myself up in the blue making that blip on the screen. But it did me no good. I hate planes. Even now I sweat like a pig when I fly.

There was a time when I was what my granddaughter would call a real airhead. Every half hour the radar screen would dissolve, and I'd be walking the beach with a girl in a long white dress and nothing underneath. But once I had subordinates, I couldn't afford to have daydreams. I told myself, "No more." And they stopped, just like that.

If you want a visionary, Fred Winslow was your man. He never talked money, it was always "the economy." Every time the Democrats milked him for a couple of thousand, you couldn't speak to the man. He had the world on his mind. For ten steps down the road he was great, but when the suppliers fucked up or the natives in the shops got restless, he'd fall apart. That's where I came in; I saw that he needed a bouncer, so a bouncer I became.

We got to be friends, sort of, at least until the oil embargo cut into the company's orders and the board of directors decided they couldn't afford the luxury of vision. Winslow felt betrayed, but that's the ball game, son. If you're not going to play to win, don't complain when you lose.

In time, though, the friction wears you down. The routine, that's nothing; the disasters, they just get your blood pumping. It's the little crap that rubs you raw: the specifications that turn out wrong because a typist won't wear her glasses; the neighbors who snub your wife because your daddy rode the caboose. It's Winslow again, off on one of his idealistic flights, coming down from the clouds to say, "But this can't be of any interest to you." They collect in your gut like grains of sand, and sooner or later they dig a hole.

Take yesterday. The manager of our Canadian shop called from Victoria to tell me he'd agreed to let the union organizer arrange a vote. What did I want him to say to the men?

I said, "What?"

He said, "You told me not to get in the way."

I said, "I told you not to get in the way, I didn't tell you to hand him the fucking shop!"

Because I had shouted, he dissolved over the phone, and I ended up spending half an hour consoling him. Sheep-dip minds. I'm surrounded by sheep-dip minds.

So at eight o'clock this morning, I crawled along the coastal road toward the ferry docks, with the grackles and garbage gulls to keep me company and a little demon in my belly playing drumrolls. Then I sat breathing exhaust fumes in the usual stalled line to buy tickets for the ferry to Victoria. Today, it was one of the four-deckers: white striped with green, too big and too new. I liked the old black barge ferries with one deck you could fit maybe thirty, forty cars onto and the cabin and canteen in an enclosure in the middle, with engines so loud you couldn't hear yourself think. The new ones, you wouldn't even know you were on the water if you didn't look down.

Finally I handed over my ticket and drove across the ramp and over a deck of treaded steel plates till I met the usual high school dropout in a dirty sweatshirt, who stuck out his hand like a cop: "Where to, sir? Victoria? Third level."

I said, "Thanks," and gunned past him as far as I could go toward the debarkation end, parking next to a farm truck.

As I retrieved my coat and binoculars from the backseat, another kid came running. "You can't stay here. This section is for San Juan Island only."

I said, "You want to bet?"

Indigent young parking attendants do not trouble sixty-year-old men in eight-hundred-dollar suits. An older hand waved him off, and I climbed the ribbed steps to the passenger deck feeling almost human.

I found a place near the windows and treated my stom-

ach to a cup of apple juice to sit on top of the morning's
Cream of Wheat and canned peach. That's my breakfast
nowadays, though occasionally I risk tea. About a year
ago the company doctor discovered I had ulcers and put
me on a diet, which I obeyed on odd Tuesdays, and a few
months later one struck blood. An ambulance rushed me
to the University Hospital. My wife was in hysterics, and
I was grinning like a fool because I'd lost so much blood.
It was touch and go the first two days, but luckily I sur-
vived, minus eight inches of something I couldn't pro-
nounce anyway.

During my recovery, my granddaughter gave me a copy
of Jaeger's *Birds of Prey* because she's a sweet girl who
loves her grandpa, and because she figured, The old man
is illiterate, better buy him a picture book. Normally I'd
have dropped it on the nightstand and forgotten about it,
but with so many people in and out and the TV on—and
it's a teaching hospital, you know, so they bring the kiddies around to stare at your belly—it was the only privacy
I could find.

I read the book. Now I don't bother with it because, in
terms of useful information, Jaeger doesn't know a hawk
from a handsaw. But while I lay on my back in the midst
of all those tubes and machines and that antiseptic smell,
it was sanity. No pretense, no lies, no girl up to her neck
in white cooing, "It's time for our enema." Just wings and
claws. As I leafed through, the day she brought it, a series
of photographs caught my eye: a bald eagle plunging from
the top of his stoop toward a terrified osprey, who drops
his catch, and *whoosh!* The old plunderer grabs that fish
before it touches the water. An amazing group of pictures! Hilarious and beautiful. I wanted to hire that bird.

When you're nearly sick to death, you begin to see
yourself from the other side of the desk, so to speak, and
wonder, who is that man? With me, that feeling got tied
up with the book. Who are these strange creatures? I

wanted to know. And then the doctors kept telling me, "Do something you don't get paid for."

My wife, noticing how much time I spent with the bird book, thought she'd get me to read. I've got nothing against reading. My father, he couldn't keep his nose out of a book. He'd read in the jakes. But I don't care for it. Books are like daydreams, they take your feet out from under you. When I sit down to a Ross Macdonald, I'm lost for the afternoon. I'll read the damned thing cover to cover, but when I stop, it's all gone: those people and the things they did to each other. That irritates me. Birds may be crazy, but they're real. You pluck them, they holler.

So I took up birding instead, and because of the ulcers, no one laughed at me. The board of directors encouraged me, even my wife approved as long as I dressed warmly. When I would hike with my binoculars around Fort Lawton, the sand in my gut would dissolve. I'd be floating with the grebes and flying with the terns, and it was no dream, just a bit of magnification.

Which makes me different, I guess, but not really. Birding doesn't turn me into Mr. Flutterby. What's new is that other world. You don't leave it behind when you drop the glasses; you carry it with you. Now I'm always hearing and seeing things that other people don't. Driving east with a customer, I'll say something like "Surf scoter. Wonder what she's doing inland." And he'll look at me as if he smelled a fart. So I've learned to hide that part of my life.

On the enclosed deck of the ferry, I was assessing my man in Victoria. We've known each other maybe twenty years. He was one of my machinists in Tacoma, where we made parts for landing gears. Bright guy, but everything his own way. Once he was turning bearings—a delicate job because they have to be accurate within a few microns—and he was buzzing them out twice as fast as he should have been.

I said, "Where's your micrometer?"

He pointed to his box.

"How the hell do you measure them?"

"Eye."

I said, "You use that micrometer or I'll screw your head around and let you eye your ass! If that bearing goes, the whole wheel assembly can collapse. 707 comes down—I'll be damned, where'd the wheels go? What do I tell the relatives? That it looked right?"

He's a lucky man. If one of those bearings had been off, I'd have canned his hide. But he was a fine machinist, and he's a good shop manager, too. Keeps the work moving, gets along with the men better than I ever did. He just needs a friendly kick in the pants now and again to let him know where his priorities are.

The bow horn jolted me back. The ferry slipped from the dock, heading north. About two-thirds of the passenger deck was enclosed—from the stern to where the spray stops in bad weather—and the enclosure was windowed all around. There was a bar and canteen at the back and more food at a big kiosk near the central steps. Otherwise the space looked like your regulation Legion hall, except for the plastic chairs riveted to the floor. At intervals there were doors to the walkway outside and, up front, two sets of doors to the bow, where fools like me freeze their butts off staring at birds or whatever.

I got up to throw away my cup. This time of day there are lots of suits in the crowd, mostly young—salesmen and buyers watching each other like thieves, workmen for the few island industries, families coming home from a weekend in the States—plus a few old men with fishing rods. I bought a newspaper, but I was too balled up to read it.

Across the aisle sat an iron-haired lady knitting a square of God knows what with strands of red and gray yarn that she tugged out of a plastic bag on the chair beside her. I asked her what she was making, but she just looked straight ahead as if there were a TV hanging from the column behind my head. Knit, knit, knit—a few minutes of that and my guts felt as if they'd been twisted into tiny knots, so I paced the deck, watching the young people check each other out.

It was spring. Everybody looked secretive. The girls bounced their knees to rhythms no one else could hear, while the boys chewed at their lower lips as though they were toughing out cramps. I wondered when one of those antsy little pricks would wander into my office, lay his briefcase on my desk, and say, "Sorry, you're in my chair." It had to happen someday. And then I'm the dope in the mariner's cap snoring over a tackle box. It would be a long time yet, I thought, but a sour burp told me not to be so sure.

We were coming up on the south end of Whidbey Island, rocking the pleasure boats in our wake and trailed by a committee of glaucous-winged gulls. Whidbey is the largest of the islands, about half as long as the Sound itself, thin and dog-legged with a long ridge running down the middle of it like a spine: pretty, but not a great nesting place for birds. The dock came into sight, and instantly every kid on the boat was through the doors and hanging over the rail.

I waited to walk out until we were under way again and the kids were back, vrooming into whatever they imagined to be a dock. There was a knuckle of rock not far from the island that's always covered with birds. I'd seen a black oystercatcher there last fall under a shelf of rock near the water. The wind bit through my suit jacket, and the glare from the water was blinding me in spite of my binoculars. I had to use the polarizing filters. Today it was terns and gulls—California gulls, mew gulls, western gulls, Bonaparte's gulls. No sign of my oystercatcher. The best I could do was an oclit.

A mew gull was nesting on one side of a rock, while her mate was in a brawl with the neighbors on the other. She couldn't see, so she stood; but instinct told her to sit, so she sat. Then curiosity got the better of her, and she flew up onto the rock, but instinct pulled her down again. She kept that up until I was out of range, and I laughed so long my mouth tasted of salt from the spray.

It was a typical Seattle morning: light blue sky, scattered clouds, and a sun that promised warmth but didn't always keep its promises. A few old farts like myself wandered the open deck. A girl in a field jacket sat sprawled on a hard plastic chair next to me as if she were lying on a chaise longue. I thought, how can their backs stand it?

She acknowledged me with a wide, lazy smile. Her blond hair glowed almost white in the morning sun. "What were you laughing at?" she asked.

"Birds."

She raveled herself out of the chair, jacket across her shoulders, hands in the pockets of her jeans. Her blouse was as thin as gauze, and there wasn't a thing underneath that wasn't her. I managed to look her in the eye, but I don't recall what color her eyes were.

I told her about the mew gull, and she asked to see. I gave her the glasses. By then you couldn't have seen the rock, much less the bird, but I gave her the glasses anyway. I thought, get a hold on yourself. It's just a pair of tits. You've seen tits before.

"It's dark," she complained.

"It's supposed to be dark." I explained about polarized light. "Come dusk, I flip this and get what they call a twilight factor. It doubles the available light. You can see till sundown."

"Expensive?"

"What do you think?"

She made a feint at throwing the binoculars overboard and handed them back. "You didn't even blink."

"It's against my religion."

Her face was pale and featureless except for her mouth, which was cut thick and reminded me of farm girls and haylofts. We walked along the railing to the stern and back the other way. I told her the story of my ulcer and described how we manufacture drill bits for oil rigs, and she listened with a smug little grin that made me uneasy. On the port side, we could see Fort Warden, and beyond it, Dungeness Spit and the strait curtained by the morning mist. A black silhouette circled overhead.

"Bonaparte's gull."

She shook her head. "Kittiwake."

When I trained the binoculars on it, damned if she wasn't right—black wingtips cut straight back. "How could you tell?"

She squeezed my forearm by way of indicating the glasses. "You mean without a whatzit factor? I grew up in the woods—my parents kind of dropped out in the seventies. I've lived around birds all my life."

At her touch, the blood burned in my face. I lectured myself, You're gray, you've got a chunk out of your gut, three root canals, and a wife who loves you. Act your age. Which worked, sort of, but my balls were singing.

She said, "I know of a nesting pair of bald eagles."

"Where?"

"San Juan Island."

"They're gone by now. Most of them fly north to breed."

"Not these. She's had eggs, and she and her mate have been taking turns sitting on them. It's an old nest in a big hemlock—it's been there forever, but this year we've had eagles. Their first brood, I think. They don't look too sure of themselves."

It was possible. A few always stayed south, and the island is lousy with rabbits.

"I could take you there."

That brought me down to earth in a hurry. I mean, how many half-naked girls take strange men into the woods to show them birds?

The invitation was tempting. A pair of eagles stay with the same nest for years, adding layer after layer of sticks and grass and chicken feathers till a storm destroys it or the limbs underneath snap from the weight. If I found their nest, I could return to watch that pair and their broods, probably for the rest of my life.

The sight of that pretty, bare flesh made her offer somehow sinister. Like a shaved head, it was a message —calculated, I suspected, to mock the feelings it aroused, whatever they happened to be.

"I can't go crashing through the underbrush in a suit," I said.

No answer.

"Do you have a phone?"

She pulled the jacket tight around her. "Not today."

Which put me right where I belonged. We leaned over the bow rail and felt a light mist in our faces. I thought about the kittiwake.

The children banged through the door and surrounded us. We were approaching Decatur Island dock, which is just that—a dock with a lot alongside a blacktop. A short, uneven line of cars waited.

I asked the girl, "You want a Coke?"

"Sure." Her lips barely moved.

On the enclosed deck, I felt the cold. My face and hands burned. After the clean salt air, the deck smelled stale, like a fish wharf hosed down for the night. The insiders were beginning to show their boredom; they paced near the windows or slouched and stared at their shoes, but the iron-haired lady sat ramrod stiff as if she were welded to her chair. Apparently she'd had enough of knitting for a while. She snapped the yarn violently and stuffed the piece into her bag. The glance she gave me as I passed could have frozen oil.

I got tea and a Coke from the Indian working the canteen and dunked the tea bag. What was I afraid of? The Victoria shop could survive another day. The organizer would make his pitch. I'd arrive tomorrow, listen to the men's gripes, reassure their wallets, and remind them that good machinists are not hard to find. That would be that, or I'd damn well hire some new ones. Today or tomorrow, it was no big deal.

When I returned she was still at the railing, her hands cupping her eyes. I noticed small things: the field jacket was ragged at the sleeves, the soles of her boots were edged with mud, and on her left hip the tip of a knife sheath was poking out from under the jacket.

"What are you looking at?" I asked.

"The water." She took the cup. "If you don't look away, after a while it begins to play on top of the light."

I tried, but I couldn't see what she was talking about. "What's the knife for?"

She grinned. "Afraid?"

"No. I just don't know many girls who carry eight-inch knives."

"You should get out more." She unsnapped it and held it under my nose. The blade had been sharpened down to the width of the handle and had the splotchy look of blades that have been used a lot. "I skin rabbits, I scale fish. Do any of your girls do that?"

I shook my head, and she sheathed the knife.

"You wouldn't know an eagle if it shit on you," she said.

"I wouldn't stand where it could."

She took the empty cup from me, lightly, without touching, pressed it into her own, and threw them both into a can nearby. "Change your mind?"

Once more the kids burst through the doors, but they didn't hang on the rail. Now it was just for the fun of running and screaming. Lopez Island lay ahead, fat and green as a lizard in the sun with San Juan hidden behind it. The morning wasn't warm yet, but at least it had stopped being cold. The haze had burned off. I could see Victoria like a black line penciled on the horizon. I felt slow and easy in the half warmth, planning the calls I'd need to make from Friday Harbor. Loons floated on the water like small black buoys with waves rolling under them. Lopez Island rose to meet us, and the gulls followed us in. For a time my body disappeared, and I was part gull, part water, part island. When we landed, two cars drove on and one elderly fisherman hobbled down the gangplank. The people who'd been staring at their shoes wandered onto the open deck to glare at the dock, as though they couldn't understand how, after coming all this way, there wasn't more to see than an island surrounded by water. As the ferry churned back into the sound, the girl shrugged off her field jacket, stretched from the rail like a dancer, and squinted at the sky as if it were a frosted window and she could see shadows on the other side. The blouse fluttered around the bare skin of her belly. Faces turned. I could imagine what they thought of me.

"Isn't it terrific?" she cried. And the crowd faded into the background like so much traffic noise.

It *was* terrific: the pine smell, the water growing bluer by the second, and her arm alongside mine on the rail. On the shingle beneath a low scarp, a great blue heron stood on his platform of sticks, nodding like a priest. San Juan Island appeared gradually around land's end—a low, wide, unspectacular version of Lopez.

We talked off and on, a lazy conversation that melted in midsentence. I tried to find out more about her—her parents, how she lived—but she deflected my questions.

Finally I figured, to hell with tact. "What do you want from me?"

She grimaced. "I have to want something?"

"Yes."

She tapped the dried mud off one of her boots against

a stanchion. Her breasts were small, the tiny nipples almost indistinguishable beneath the cloth.

"Okay, those." She pointed to the binoculars.

"Too much."

"I might forget where the eagles are."

"And I might find them on my own."

That seemed to amuse her. "How about a knife? Not like this one—a Gerber, six-inch blade."

"No problem."

"You're sure?" The girl was no bargainer.

"I'm sure."

In the easy silence of people who have struck a deal, we watched the island grow. Friday Harbor rose up from the shoreline. Patches of trees and pasture alternated over low hills. I could see cattle grazing.

She pulled on the olive drab and retrieved her knapsack. I followed along the rail. "It's not far from the road," she said. "You won't even scuff your shoes."

A glaze of sunlight rode the surface of the water. A floating grebe stirred in our wake and settled back.

The kid who'd chased my car leaned against the wall of the enclosed deck to warn those going below. "Watch it, now. Hold on, those steps are slippery."

When he saw her, he whistled through his teeth. " 'Lo, sweetheart. Where've you been?"

She slung the pack over her shoulder.

"What have you got there, huh? Something for me?" He made a feint at the skirts of her jacket, but with a furious little snarl she bolted past him and down the stairs. He grinned at me as if we were old friends. "Moonchild of the islands. She read your palm?"

The grin pissed me off. "You've got a problem, son."

"Me? I don't have problems. I stay away from them."

"Do you always make grabs at your passengers?"

"People complain that she talks crazy, that she doesn't act decent. I have to check it out." He pulled a cigarette pack from the pocket of the sweatshirt and tapped one against a wrist the color of dead fish. "In Friday Harbor, they say she'll fuck anything in pants. Put pants on a horse, she'll fuck the horse." His grin widened into a smirk. "Then if she doesn't like it, she cuts your dick off. That's what I hear."

"What's your name? I'm going to report you." I was so furious, the words came out in a whisper.

"Underwood. Rex Underwood. Go ahead, sir. Tell them all about it."

If there hadn't been so many people, I think I would've flattened him—or tried, anyway. "I will," I retorted, but we both knew I was lying. His wheezy laughter followed me to the deck below.

The girl had gone on, but I had to stop to catch my breath. The demon in my gut had grown claws, and I had to hold on to the passenger-side mirror of a truck to keep from pitching forward.

"Shit!" I gave the mirror a yank. It'd been a long time since anybody had mocked me like that, but it was my own fault. If you lift your ass from cover, you've got to expect some half-wit's going to salt it with buckshot.

I leaned against the door and breathed in the stink of seawater and gas. In the shadows around me were cars bound for Victoria, hunched in their stalls. San Juan Island had been cut to a strip of treetops and bright sky between the restraining wall and the deck above. I stared at a sweating steel beam between me and the wall and knew I couldn't go any farther. The mood had broken. I felt as I did years ago, when I'd glance up from a mystery to find my daughter beside my chair, waiting for the answer to a question I hadn't heard—like, if I reached out to touch her, my hand would pass right through.

In the murk of the lower deck, the plausible excursion of a few moments ago seemed unreal. The weird girl, the island, an eagles' nest hidden in the woods, were the stuff of fairy tales, where birds talk like philosophers and everybody gets changed into something else at the end. For this, I'd have to lie to my shop manager and my secretary and maybe my wife, then more lies to cover the lies.

A car roared to life below. The pain in my belly eased, and I decided to give my legs a try, skirting the edge of a long puddle that trembled with the throb of the ferry's engines. I could come back, I told myself, to find them on my own without the risk and without the lies. The smartass deckhand thundered by two steps at a time, swung around the bar at the landing, and plummeted down as if there were someone at the bottom with a stopwatch. The engines shut down, and my image materialized in the puddle, glazed with a gasoline rainbow. Soon a Jeep came up the ramp and parked nearby. A woman and two children got out. One of them sped up the stairs; the other wanted to try it on all fours, but his mother slung him over her hip. When the vibrations began again, I followed them up to the open deck.

We'd been going backward. As I came to the bow rail, the engines reversed and the boat labored past the dock. The girl stood at the edge of a gravel lot, a shabby creature in the uniform of another generation, her hair flaming behind her in the breeze. She saw me and turned away.

The sky seemed to fade to a paler blue to compensate for the blue the water was becoming, and Victoria was a black ziggurat at the edge of a spit of gray. As we rumbled beyond the western tip of the island, I found a seat and pondered the dark splotch my body threw across the deck. There were a few puzzled glances—I'd like to think that I spoiled somebody's fun. But I was too tired to take much pleasure in it. I just wanted to feel the sun on my face.

When a shadow crossed the bow, I closed my eyes,

closed them and laughed. He was circling our leeward side, calling "kak-kak-kak" to warn us off: a young male eagle, irritated that we'd interrupted his fishing. His head and tail were so white, I could make them out plainly against that feeble sky. His black wings rippled. I thought, You son of a bitch, you beautiful, dumb son of a bitch.

People were shouting and shielding their eyes with magazines. A woman with a camera called to him the way you'd call a dog. He swooped and shrieked, herding us into deep water. Then he turned back, gliding low, his wings stretched from one end of the island to the other, as if it were something he'd just built and he was packing in the loose earth. Finally he paused, perfectly still. A draft caught him, and he soared in a wide arc over Friday Harbor and rowed eastward into the heart of the island.

Hot Fudge

Tonguing the unlit cigar from one side of his mouth to the other, Marion Elder waited for his brother-in-law's laughter to trail off. The freckled, dirty-nailed hand held out a china swan, whose hollow body was filled with chunks of fudge.

"Good for what ails you."

Marion shook his head, and the freckled face above him grinned.

"Remember what Grandpa Charlie used to say. Whiskey, women, and fudge candy are what make life worth living, and if he'd had to give up one of them, it wouldn't have been the fudge."

"No thanks."

Marion studied his reflection in the mirror that the night had made of Arthur Frisch's picture window: still slim at forty-eight, his salt-and-pepper hair crew cut, his eyes hidden in the shadow of overhanging brows. This last gave his face a slightly apelike expression, which he had never quite accepted as being his. He knew that his brother-in-law was baiting him. It had been going on ever since Arthur married Ellen and would probably continue till one of them was in his grave, for Marion was an abstemious man, a man of principle and proud of it. He never drank strong liquor, seldom ate sweets, and disapproved of speaking about women in terms of appetite; and in that rectitude Arthur found an endless source of amusement which at times would border on rage.

Still, Marion was a patient man, and he was not going

to allow himself to be deflected from the point of his visit.

"Deborah's worried," he said to Arthur's reflection, pacing the room.

The squat man stopped and ran a hand over the gray haze that remained atop his bald head. "Don't let's start on that again."

But Marion had orders from home to take the subject as far as it could go. "Sooner or later . . . "

"Deborah's not taking care of her, I am," Arthur said. "Ellen is."

With a little "hah" of annoyance, Arthur threw himself into an overstuffed chair facing his sister's husband. "I don't hear Ellen complaining."

Marion gnawed placidly on his cigar.

On the couch between them, her back humped from age, sat a frail old woman with a patchwork comforter over her legs and a Chicago Cubs baseball cap on her head, rocking and whispering to herself. One arm lay on top of the comforter, as light and dry as a snakeskin.

"Look at her," Marion pursued. "She doesn't know what's going on right in front of her. She sees nothing but shadows, she can't hear me unless I scream, and what the diabetes allows her to eat, her blood pressure won't. She doesn't need you, she needs doctors and nurses and people who know what the hell they're doing."

Arthur glanced silently out the window, across the gravel road and over the plowed-under fields to where the interstate began its slow curve west of Bloomington. The Thanksgiving-eve traffic edged along like a string of white-eyed ants.

"She knows more than she lets on," he said.

"She doesn't even know what day it is."

"So? Neither do I half the time."

Arthur hated arguments. Most people had reasons, but Arthur seldom knew what his reasons were, and even when he did, like now, he couldn't make sense of them to anyone. The man was right, as far as right went. This woman was not the grandmother he had known all his life. The Olga Frisch who'd won prizes solving the double acrostics in the *Chicago Daily News,* who'd put custard in her rhubarb pies and had shown him, when he was little, how to make sour apples sweet by putting salt on them; the woman who, told that her son and his wife had been killed at a railroad crossing, had cried like a maniac for an hour, then went out and beheaded a hen for supper—that woman was gone and in her place was a stranger. Even when she spoke of her past, it sounded as if she were recalling a woman long dead.

But there were places right did not go. The last three years, she'd been sleeping downstairs in her great-grandson Gordon's old bedroom, and though she often couldn't remember her own last name, every Saturday (if she somehow found out it was Saturday) she'd make one of the family help her upstairs to her room, so she could go through the motions of dusting and changing the sheets on the four-poster her husband had died in. To Deborah this was another sign of senility, but for Arthur it had a kind of sentimental poetry that he felt called upon to defend. As long as she could make that absurd, painful trek, he could not let go of her.

"She ought to live her own way so long as she can," he said.

Marion removed the cigar from his mouth, sized the mangled butt with one eye, then bit off the end and spat it into the ashtray.

"There's a burnt-up pan in the trash. I suppose she turned on the stove again."

Arthur didn't answer. Watching the old woman, he realized there was a cadence to her movements. He wondered if she were praying or singing or what.

"You know, one of these times, living her own way, she's going to burn your house down."

"I'll take that chance."

Marion snorted. "She's still got a bruise from that fall she took a couple of months ago, trying to reach God knows what out of the cupboard. Next time she'll break her hip."

"I'll take that chance, too."

As if by arrangement, they let the argument lapse. A taint of sarcasm had begun to color the conversation, and both men preferred to back off. Marion returned to the reflection in the window: Ellen's big Hammond organ guarded the door to the kitchen; a console color TV sprawled near Arthur's chair, with framed pictures of children and grandchildren strewn over the top; on the hardwood-paneled wall hung a sunburst clock, deformed by a swell in the glass; and beneath it, the old woman on the couch.

Useless, he thought. The stubbornness of a wayward man trying to act responsibly. Marion had done what he could. If there were a tragedy, the blame would not fall on him.

Having cleared the matter from his mind, Marion again appraised the organ, the TV, and the hardwood paneling and pondered the mystery of God's disposition of worldly goods. He, who had worked at least as hard as his brother-in-law, had sacrificed more, had been shrewd in calculating the markets, at shifting from one commodity to another, and who had prayed for guidance in all things —he had little to show that wouldn't go into next year's planting; where Arthur, who had stuck to hogs and beans for twenty years because he didn't understand anything else, was rolling in money. Much as Marion might wish to console himself that to God these things were no more than reflections in a window, it was bitter to see all that cherrywood on the walls of a man with no sense, especially the man who had gotten around Ellen Brannon.

Meanwhile, Arthur slouched in his chair and worried that he might be wrong. He was insensitive, he knew.

Everybody said it. All his life a faint cloud of disapproba-
tion had followed him. Daydreamer, they whispered.
Clown. The child who had never been spanked became
the willful young man who had hung around Bloomington
bars and flunked out of college and gone to work for a
grain elevator and, one rainy Monday at ten in the morning, had married Ellen Brannon in the huge fan-shaped
sanctuary of the Second Presbyterian Church with six
friends in front pews (no Brannons among them) and his
father as best man, and had then fought his father over a
piece of land, moved to Morton, Illinois, to work for Caterpillar, and later walked out of his parents' funeral when
he imagined the preacher had insulted him. That was his
story. There were others that could have been made of
his life, but this was the one he was known by and believed.

Marion was not the only man with whom he shared
silences. Arthur had a habit, even with those he loved, of
punctuating his impulses with sudden retreats, of closing
up like a sow bug whenever he felt exposed. People who
wanted to get through to him, he knew, talked to Ellen,
because Ellen was the only one who could influence him
once he'd made up his mind—another role he'd forced
upon her without asking. He believed he was a fool but
could not bring himself to feel regret, only a faint remorse
that he wasn't a better man. After all, he had been lucky.
Through the reflection on the window, he contemplated
the glaze of moonlight on the corn stubble in the field
across the road—a no-man's-land of broken stalks cut
across by the dark scar of a slough.

In midarc, Granny Frisch stopped and lifted her head
as if she'd heard something. "Arthur?"

Heaving himself out of his chair, he straddled the coffee
table to get close enough. "What do you want, lover?"

She looked disappointed. "I'm cold."

"Want your shawl?"

She didn't respond. When he slipped the shawl over her shoulders, she let it hang.

"Lord, I thought I'd never get that man off the phone!"

It was any Illinois farm woman's voice—nasal, full of round r's, hoarse from years in the weather—but Marion sat up like a shot.

"Reverend Laesch," Ellen explained, dropping her glasses onto the frilled bodice of her blouse, where they dangled from a silver chain.

"Wants you to play for some damned fool thing," her husband finished.

"A wedding. I told him I'd think about it."

"When was the last time you said no?"

Instead of replying, she leaned over the back of the couch and rearranged the old woman's shawl. Ellen carried enough weight on her now to make bending a bit awkward, and as she picked and tucked, the flesh swung beneath her arms, but her eyes shone like the eyes of a secretive child. She smiled toward Marion, who was putting on his jacket. Her voice, like the hand she laid upon his arm, betrayed the slightly guilty poise of a woman who had been loved all her life for reasons she has never been able to fathom.

"My, aren't we impatient. Did you get the card table and chairs?"

"In the pickup," Marion said.

"Then don't leave so soon."

"Things to do," he laughed, uneasy under her touch. "No rest for the wicked."

They followed him out through the new kitchen and the shabby back hall where their work clothes hung on pegs, down the flimsy back steps where two pairs of muddy boots lay jumbled together, into the backyard and the smell of pig.

Ellen crossed her arms against the breeze. "Tell Deb I'll call her in the morning, around seven."

He nodded.

"What happened to Chuckie? She told me she was sending Chuck, and you show up."

"He was supposed to come straight home from basketball practice." Marion slammed the gate behind him so hard the hog wire hummed down the line.

Ellen chortled. "Don't be such a stick. She's sweet."

"Sweet!" It was the cry of a stepped-on dog. "There's no father, there's no money, the mother works the night shift in a hospital in Normal, leaves the girl and her sister alone in the house. And they say when she's home there are so many men in and out you'd think it was a barbershop."

His voice got more shrill as he went on, and he squeezed the rusty fleur-de-lis that ornamented the top of the gate as if he intended to pluck it off. The fear of the girl had been building ever since he'd seen them outside the movie theater: her head resting easy against his son's chest and Chuck's hand drawing little circles on her ass.

"We should have whupped Larry Otto when he put up those prefabs. Now we've got trash from the city in our schools." It wasn't the sex that worried him. Those scruples had quickly fallen away in the face of a greater threat: this was the sort of girl who could bring a man down and steal his future. Married to a girl like that, a boy might not get through college, might not play enough baseball for the scouts to notice him, might not, in other words, make something more of himself than a farmer. But you couldn't ask Arthur and Ellen to understand that. "Can't tell what might happen."

"She seems nice enough," Ellen protested. "She sings in church."

Which deflated him a bit. Marion wiped the rust from his hands. "It's not the girl, not her fault. It's . . . " But he could not say whose fault it was. "I just hope she doesn't give him something he can't walk away from."

Arthur slipped an arm around his wife's waist. "Hell, you know how that puppy stuff goes. Sooner or later, something will come up between them."

"I pray for it," Marion sighed.

Again, the old woman started and raised her head as though she were listening.

"Arthur?"

No one answered.

"Arthur?"

She let the shawl drop behind her and set aside the black purse on her lap.

"Arthur?"

Carefully balanced between the coffee table and the couch, she lowered herself, arms trembling, onto her knees, then crawled in the space between the furniture, dragging her purse and patting the table with her free hand till it fell on the china swan. With a yip of joy she opened her purse and probed inside, sorting by feel the coupons and phone numbers she'd saved but could not read; then she slipped in one, two—considered the risks —three chunks of fudge and, red-faced from the strain, climbed laboriously back onto the couch, panting in triumph.

They watched Marion's pickup skid from the lane onto the gravel road, spinning a cloud of dust across the face of the moon.

" 'Can't tell what might happen,' " Arthur mimicked. "What a prick."

"If you can't govern your tongue, something's going to come up between us."

Arthur squeezed the roll of flesh that swelled over the elastic of her slacks. "I'll pray for it."

. . .

Driving the county road home, Marion Elder pondered the murk ahead, where the fields flooded into the night sky, and the changes in his son. The boy had been born with his father's build, his father's brows, and as he grew, had taken on his father's quiet tenacity. By twelve he had read his father's Scott and Twain and still furtively loved Dr. Doolittle, and had begun to express his father's ideals with a tongue-tied passion that amused his listeners and embarrassed Marion as much as it pleased him. So alike were they that Marion had never paused to consider whether they were actually close. Come high school, the boy had filled out. There was more cheek than brow, and people said he looked like his mother. The boy hardly seemed to care for anything except his car. He went through the motions in school and even in sports, the way he did at home, making an insolence out of obeying. Open rebellion would have been easier for this father to take, but rebellion would have demanded guts, and he doubted Chuck had much of that commodity. He just curled up in the cave he had made of himself, sneering at praise and welcoming punishment for the excuse it gave him not to come out.

Beyond the railroad crossing where his wife's parents had been killed, Marion made a turn and then another at a corner presided over by three grain elevators, which took him past the darkened high school.

There was no use laying blame. At one time or another he'd faulted himself, Deborah, the school, television, and now the girl for his son's behavior—but the indictments always fell apart. Chuck would follow his own lights. It probably didn't even matter what choices the boy made. Whether he lived out his father's dreams or wadded them up like trash, they'd always be strangers.

The road dipped to cross a creek and passed one of the

old family cemeteries that were tucked into fields throughout the Illinois countryside. There, as though he'd been meant to see it, his lights brushed a mag-wheeled blue Volkswagen, frosted with silver flames, which was parked in the weedy drive. Marion had half a mind to get the shotgun down from the rack behind his seat and send a load of buckshot over their heads. Instead, he drove on till the truck had tipped the rise, then braked violently and pounded on the steering wheel with both fists.

"Jesus Christ! Why?"

In the Volkswagen, Chuck sat back and tried to calm his breathing, aware of nothing but the knot in his belly and the body of the girl beside him. Head down but still turned toward him, her blouse open, one breast silver white in the moonlight. Her jeans were unzipped, showing a white triangle of panties and a dark tuft of hair above the elastic. Gradually he realized that her head was down because she was crying, and he hated himself but said nothing. The scent of her was everywhere. Suddenly he pounded the steering wheel with both fists.

"Why not?"

11

TH E outbuildings were separated from the house by a blacktop and looked abandoned. The red barn had gone purple with age, and there were flamelike gashes in the wall where the wood had rotted out. The silo leaned away from it as though contact might compromise its reputation. The unused crib had collapsed, and the corrugated-steel machine shed had bowed in the middle. Yet only a stranger would have taken this decay as a sign of poverty. Some of the richest farmers in the county had barns that looked no better. The house, too, had weathered down to gray wood in spots, but Marion refused to paint it because painting would raise his property taxes. It was a crime, he said, to tax a man for keeping up his property.

The weatherman, God's chief representative on earth, had provided an Indian summer day for Thanksgiving, warm enough for shirtsleeves. The air was clear, and you could see for miles. In his yard the children were playing keep-away with a small rubber football, using the trunk of an old oak as an obstacle. Since there hadn't been any rain lately, the tree still carried its dead leaves, and some of them had kept their color. Gordon's youngest girl, Ginny, leapt and brought down dead leaves from a drooping branch and showered them over the others as if they were money. There was an owl's nest near the top older than any of them. As a boy Chuck had stood under that tree and shot at the nest with a hand-me-down .22. The owls had retaliated by littering the yard with bloody cat fluff.

A car thundered by like a mechanized hailstorm and honked as it passed. Linda Frisch and Peggy Frisch Nafziger waved from the porch steps. The movement disturbed Peggy's eighteen-month-old son, Arthur, who had been contemplating a one-eyed cat hunched between two bushes. He yanked at his mother's blouse, and automatically, without looking down, she pried his hand away and kissed it. When he mewled in protest, her body began to rock.

"Sounds like nap time," she said.

Through the window screen, swelled like a sail from years of northwest wind, Chuck watched the baby mouthing its mother's blouse and felt a tiny flame run up his spine. The men were sitting around the TV, waiting for

the football game to begin and arguing about the weather
—thoughtfully, almost angrily, as if it were something
that could be settled between them.

"But we've got to have rain the next couple of weeks, a
long, steady one," Dwight Cooper whined. Even in good
times, his uncle's voice set Chuck's teeth on edge. Since
the drought had come, Dwight sounded like a band saw.
"If we don't, I'll be drinking out of the septic tank."

"Always thought your water tasted funny," Arthur said,
and the men laughed.

Billy Nafziger didn't bother to hide his distaste. "Why
make a big to-do out of it? The water table's not that low.
Rain'll come when it comes."

"Long as we get snow this winter," Marion yawned,
"we'll do fine."

Chuck felt like putting his fist through the screen. Their
talk was stupid, their laughter was stupid, and so were
they. So were the women in the kitchen. Like the land
that stretched out from this barely perceptible high
ground to the horizon, they were as flat and predictable
as the wall of a factory. The same opinions, the same
complaints, the same jokes he'd heard all his life—and
they kept using that sameness on him like a hobble to
keep him in place. He hated them and hated himself for
feeling that way, but they never changed, and every
morning he woke up different—older and, in some ways,
more frightening to himself—and the older he got, the
more childish they seemed.

The long front room was divided by simple arrange-
ments of furniture on either side of the door—to his right,
a living room in which every chair and sofa angled slightly
toward the television, and to his left, a dining room presided over by an antique breakfront whose cut-glass windows spread rainbows over the dishes inside. Behind him
was the table he and his father had stretched to twice its
usual length, around which they had placed every variety
of chair known to man; and which his mother had cov-

ered with a soft, patterned cloth and set with gold-rimmed china and silverware, then proceeded to spoil by running strips of black and orange crepe down the center and putting candle pilgrims and turkeys, paper pump-kins, and pinecones on top. And the women, when they arrived, had said, "Oh, how sweet!" as if they'd never seen anything so pretty in their lives, making Chuck feel like the only honest person in the room and yet making him wonder if this weren't the kind of honesty that could cripple a man.

They said he had promise in exactly the same tone they had said, "How sweet," as though he were in the same league with the wax pilgrims. Sure, he had promise. Here. Where the woman who missed the fewest notes played the church organ and a boy six feet two could make it at forward. Anywhere else they would see he had nothing—no talent, no smarts, just relatives. When he got older he'd probably be the dullest one of the bunch, if he didn't step off into darkness.

Stepping off into darkness was what Reverend Laesch called it when a man was ruled by his passions. The pictures he drew of what happened then—of driving out of control, of drowning—had struck the boy deeply because they were images he'd already met in his dreams. He suspected that he was in danger of losing his soul. Even in church he could not keep his passions from mastering him. An old woman like his aunt Ellen could make his ears burn just by touching his arm. His dreams were full of car crashes and dark figures with guns, of blood and dismemberment. He knew they were connected to Holly because when he dreamed of making love to her, he could feel his soul escaping. Sometimes it didn't return, and he'd feel as empty as he did when he looked at the land. Other times he woke up to wet sheets and a panicky pleasure, knowing he could not hide them from his mother.

"Okay, champ! Okay!" Peggy Frisch Nafziger laughed.

Cradling the baby in one arm, she undid the buttons of her blouse, then unclasped her nursing bra and pressed the wide brown nipple between two fingers. Even before his mouth touched her breast, the baby had begun to suck.

Chuck's face burned, but despite his shame, he couldn't turn his eyes away or keep his flesh from rising. Even this, he thought, feeling the familiar combination of warmth and despair. Even this.

"Chuckie!"

His mother's voice. He turned away from the door but couldn't walk without betraying himself, so he stood there like an idiot, furious at himself for his weakness.

"Chuck! Come here a second!"

He stayed where he was, feebly pretending to rearrange the table decorations. Slowly, it began to ease.

"Chuck Elder! You heard your mother. Get your butt in that kitchen and find out what she wants," Marion yelled.

His eyes rose to meet his father's, but it was his father who looked away first. I could break you in half, he thought.

Deborah Elder poured Triscuits into a basket lined with a white cloth napkin, and beside it she put a crockery jar of cheese spread, whose label she had scraped off the night before. The other women leaned against the counter to take the weight off their legs and nibbled cashews from a Venus-shell dish as they rummaged through the past—who from back then was doing what now, and wasn't it just like him? There was no act so foolish or remarkable or chance-ridden that they did not, in the end, discover it to have been just like him.

Her son shambled in, hunched over like a thief, and Deborah tried to remember what she'd wanted him to do. But the anger in his look and his mow of uncombed hair had stolen her memory.

"My word, Chuck! Stand up straight. The girls won't want to be seen with you if you walk around like something that escaped from the circus."

She knew that there was only one girl, had even met her, but in conversation she always spoke as though there were numberless girls, none in particular.

Since Marion had made such a fuss to get him in here, Deborah couldn't say she'd forgotten why, so she asked him to reach down a jar of preserves, which he did by leaning his six-foot-something frame nearly on top of Grandma in her chair and tossing the jar back over his shoulder. It would have hit her in the face if Ellen hadn't caught it. Before Deborah could gather her wits to say what she thought of that, he'd grabbed a handful of cashews and was out the door.

The women were smiling—Marion's sister, Beth, and his mother and Ellen, who was rolling the jar of preserves from one hand to the other.

"I sometimes wonder if it was worth the effort," Deborah sighed.

The other two murmured sympathetically, but Ellen's smile became more secretive.

"I'll find something to put these in," she said.

Martha Elder and her daughter picked up where their conversation had left off. Freed from their gaze, Deborah patted a loose strand of hair into place. Ellen was truly unforgivable, she thought. Always the superior smile that suggested you were a joke she alone understood. Deborah could hear her in the other room playing up to the men. Fat as a horse, and the men still gathered around her with a doggy sort of persistence, the way they had in the days when she was seducing Arthur. Everybody said she was a saint because of Grandma, but . . .

"Granny, no! Good God!"

The old woman had swung herself sidesaddle on the folding chair and had nearly tipped over. In a single, violent motion, Deborah dragged her grandmother's legs around to the front and centered her rear end; then she grabbed the old woman's hands and pinned them to her thighs.

"Don't do that! If you want up, ask one of us. Okay? Okay? Do you want to go to the bathroom?"

Through her thick lenses, Grandma Frisch glared at her antagonist's chin as if she wanted to bite it off. Deborah glared back, hating Arthur for forcing this hazard on her. In a moment, however, her control had returned. She smiled wearily toward her in-laws, who did not smile back.

"Get your own," Ellen called back at the men as she came through the kitchen door. "The game's started," she announced, and held up a small, rose-shaped bowl for Deborah's inspection. "Good enough?"

"Of course."

"What's the matter, honey?"

Grandma was bent over, holding her purse to her stomach with both hands. Ellen reached out to her, more from habit than feeling. The old woman flinched at first, but then, recognizing the touch, relaxed and allowed her cheek to be caressed.

"Don't worry. Nobody's going to steal your purse."

"I'd better take the cheese and crackers to the men," Deborah said. "I'm going to get the dickens for being so long."

"Tell me where the nuts are, Deb, and I'll put more out."

Deborah groaned. "Did that boy eat all the cashews?"

Chuck's mind slipped off into the dark, drifting gently to the cemetery where the moon glared on his dashboard like ice.

Holly tugged his fist from the steering wheel, pried the fingers loose, and laid them against her damp cheek; he felt like crying, too, out of sheer frustration. She kissed the knuckle of his little finger, tested it with her tongue, then bit it hard enough to make him wince.

"Don't you love me?" he asked. (A hypocritical question since he'd made it a point of honor never to say "I love you," but she was crying, and he didn't want to lose the advantage.)

She threw his hand back at him. "I love you."

"Then what's the problem?"

"Not here."

"Where?"

Her gaze wandered into the tiny cemetery as though she were looking for a spot among the stones. "It's got to be—oh shit, I don't know. It's got to be pretty. Don't you understand? It's got to mean more than . . ." She was going to say "sex," but that wasn't what she meant. She just doubted he'd understand anything else. "I want us to mean something, all right? Anyway"—she tapped the low roof of the Volkswagen—"I'm not an acrobat."

Pretty. What did she mean? "When is it going to be pretty?"

His question was so dumb, it made her giggle, and the giggle turned into a cough. "Someday," she wheezed. "Maybe."

"Like when I'm gone and you're out with some other jerk."

"Maybe."

She tried to take his hand again, but he shook her off. His head was beginning to ache, and waves were breaking and receding in his stomach. "It hurts," he said.

"I know. I think it's supposed to."

"No, it's not."

When he glanced up he found her watching him with the half-solemn, half-amused expression that would

come over her whenever she had a secret she wanted
him to guess.

On the screen, Detroit's wide receiver cut between a line-
backer and a cornerback and reached across the sideline
for a pass—from the end-zone camera he reached again,
and again from the reverse angle. Each time the ball
slipped through his hands.

Deborah set the cheese and crackers on the coffee
table and, rising, pointed a finger at Chuck. "You've had
enough already!"

Marion, opposite the boy, skinned off a slim crescent of
cheese and scraped it onto a cracker.

"Who's playing?" she asked no one in particular.

"Chicago and Detroit."

Toying with one of the buttons on her beige suit, she
squinted at the TV. "Who's winning?"

"Nobody's winning," snorted Billy Nafziger. "Bears are
losing."

She squinted a while longer and finally picked up the
beer cans and retreated to the kitchen. No one had given
her the dickens. They hadn't even bothered to say,
"Thank you."

"They always were a crazy bunch," Marion's mother declared, hefting her enormous body upright on its spindly
legs. She'd been telling the others how Grandpa Charlie
had kept a still in his basement even after Prohibition.
"Liked his own better, I guess. And Arthur's father was
like him, only worse. No substance. Lots of imagination,
but not an ounce of substance. Ellen, do you remember
the plan Paul had to build helicopters in Pontiac? Helicopters! And that was before the War. According to him,
nobody was going to drive anymore; we were all going to

fly. And Arthur! I tell you, Ellen, you were a godsend to that man because he started out worse than his father. Lies! My Lord, the lies that boy told. Ask him how to get to town, and he'd send you to China. That's what was wrong between the two of them—it wasn't the land, it was too much imagination in one place."

As she washed out the empty Ball jar, Ellen wondered why people couldn't find other things to talk about. There was so much good and so much bad in the man, yet they kept worrying the same old stories like the preacher with his parables.

"It *was* the land," Ellen said. "We had some bad harvests, and Paul decided to sell the south acres. Arthur wanted the farm whole for Gordy."

"But then why would he walk out of his parents' funeral, if it was the land?" Beth countered, as if the sequence were obvious and devastating.

Because he loved them, Ellen felt like shouting, because Arthur was hurt and lonely and nobody would let him say so without judging. Instead, she answered, "The minister spoke against him."

"Maybe. . . ." Martha had been there. "Or maybe he got an idea and let it run away with him."

"Martha! The man did preach the lost sheep and the ninety and nine!"

She nodded amiably. "That he did," she said, and leaned back against the counter with a sigh.

Deborah returned to the kitchen and checked the turkey. "I think there's something wrong with the thermometer," she said.

Gray shadows shifted and settled, shifted again in the gray haze, and the voices, clear but too far away, seemed to rise to the surface, then disappear like fish. Normally the old woman could identify people by their smell or by

a sense of them that she got as they moved around her
and could cast the world accordingly, but the strong odor
of roast turkey was confusing her. She couldn't tell who
was who, and her stomach hurt. If she complained, they
would give her saltless crackers. But on a day like this
she preferred to go hungry than give in to crackers. She
ran her fingers over the cloth of her dress, letting its softness take away some of the ache.

She could tell there were strangers in the room and
wished they hadn't been invited. It was hard enough for
her to keep her mind on the moment. Now and then some
fool (usually one related to her) would break through the
surface to say something utterly mad, startling her no less
than if a bird had flown onto her shoulder and asked her
name. Their world had long since become too indistinct
to serve as more than a backdrop. The real world, the
one in which she walked and talked like any other human
being, she had to create from the past, and so her
Thanksgivings were peopled with family long dead,
friends washed away by the Depression or the War or
the weather, grandchildren and great-grandchildren
shifting about through the grayness in forms they had
long since abandoned.

In spite of the strangers blurring the landscape, it still
would be her Thanksgiving dinner. Charlie would serve,
and in between the bites of mashed potatoes Ellen would
force into her mouth, she would run to the kitchen to fill
the tureen with gravy. The fact that she was imagining it
interested her no more than the fact that she had deco-
rated her own house. As long as she was able to piece
together this makeshift present, the past would stay in
good order, and she'd know where to look for her memories when she wanted them. But a frightening change
had taken place a couple of years ago when her glaucoma
had gotten worse. More and more, the gray would steal
in without warning over her creations. She would wander

lost through her own past and come upon her memories like half-buried gravestones stumbled upon in the fog.

As her fingers clutched and released her dress, the old woman studied the one bright triangle in all that gray, which she knew must be light from a window falling on the floor, and fearful of the shadows that crossed it, she sought a memory to comfort her. Turning her head just a little, as though to gaze up at the stained-glass window that the light was streaming through, she caught Karl Frisch in a pew with his family, staring at her.

She liked Karl staring at her, but she didn't like him doing it so often in public. Which was why she couldn't return his smile and why her replies to his greetings were always shorter than she meant them to be. But now and then, he would stop by to sit on the porch with her and her parents and whoever else might be there, and she began to walk out with him. She called him Charlie because Karl sounded too German, and soon he was asking others to call him that, too. He was one of the few men she enjoyed. He was older than she. He had been in the Army and had seen other parts of the country. She liked his laughter for its impertinence, and she respected his occasional fits of melancholy because they were mysterious. Yet there was something unguarded about him that frightened her, and she was careful not to betray her feelings. Throughout that summer he had visited her, some weeks every day, some weeks not at all. He spoke of buying land near his father's farm.

It was after one of his unexplained absences, after church one autumn morning, that he had asked her, in front of her parents and all of her friends, to walk ahead with him. She could hear the laughter behind them. Charlie talked about the sermon, about the weather, about a bank loan his father would help him secure. She let her dress drag in the mud rather than reveal her trembling hands. They stopped in front of her house. He kicked at the tongue of a thresher her father had rented for harvest. Then, right there in front of everyone, he took her hand, and at the touch of that rough skin, she despised him. He was crude, he was awkward, he was ridiculous, and she hated herself for ever loving him.

She pried her hand away before he could speak, and in a panic for some explanation, she pointed down at his feet and cried, "Boots *in der Kirche!*"

Startled, he looked down in embarrassment at the boots he had so carefully polished for church that morning, and she saw with relief, then with anguish, that she had wounded him. Worse, that he had understood.

He tipped his hat silently.

The triangle disappeared, and the smell of the turkey cut through her memory like a knife. She moaned from hunger.

Beth Cooper let go of the curtain pull. "That's better."

"Beer call!" Arthur careened into the kitchen. "Lord be praised! End of the first quarter and the Bears are only down by ten. Even Marion's going to have one. Want a beer, girls?"

Martha allowed that she might have just one.

There were none in the refrigerator. Arthur peered over the top of the door at his sister, and the look that passed between them—of suspicion on one side and barely disguised gloating on the other—hadn't changed, no matter who wore which, since they were children.

"Where'd you hide the beer, Deb?"

"There was a six-pack in the fridge this morning."

"One six-pack?" Arthur leaned on the door, appraising his sister.

Recognizing his expression, Deborah smiled so brightly that, among the deep wrinkles that branched down from her mouth, her dimples appeared. "It's Thanksgiving, not New Year's Eve."

"I doubt if there's a store open from here to Bloomington," Arthur mused, still holding the door open.

"You'll survive. There's plenty of coffee and cups in the
breakfront."

"We'll see." Finally he shut the door and, in almost the
same motion, reached out and ruffled her hair.

"Arthur! Damn you!"

She was laughing and so was he.

It occurred to Martha Elder, who had watched without
the least surprise, that this was the first time she'd seen
them laugh together in ages.

Head back against the banister, Ellen let her eyes wander
over the landscape. The sky seemed almost white in the
offing. The land, like her own, went on forever, and there
was nothing in it threatening or unfamiliar. The grandchildren were in shirtsleeves; she wore a sweater because there was a nip in the air. Raising her face to the
sun, she dozed for a second and when she woke found
herself gazing into the leaves of the big oak, feeling as if
she were falling into them.

The children cried, "Grandpa," and Art appeared in
the lane, tossed back the rubber football, climbed into his
truck, and drove off.

Linda returned from the bathroom, a wet spot on the
knee of her pale green pantsuit where she had soiled it,
kneeling to listen to one of Gordy's kids. Perched lightly
on the edge of the step above Ellen's, she slipped her
hand along the underside of her thigh as though she were
straightening a skirt, and glanced down complacently into
her mother's raised face.

"Where's Daddy going?"

"I don't know."

Neither of them could think of anything to say. They
looked toward the receding puff of dust.

Linda was Ellen's youngest, her prettiest child, the one

she had lavished more care on than the other two com-
bined because she had never quite been able to like her.
Stubborn, self-pitying, and even violent as a girl, Linda
had, since she'd earned her MBA and gone to work for
Caterpillar, become a model of devotion, treating her
parents with a thoughtfulness and concern that, to Ellen,
amounted almost to condescension. In both guises the girl
had remained a mystery, though thankfully one her
mother no longer felt responsible for. In the slim girl with
her arms around her knees, Ellen could not imagine the
junior executive, the skier and gourmet cook, the girl who
once jokingly told her father that she belonged to the
man-of-the-month club. What she saw was what she had
always seen—an odd conglomeration of angles like a
scrawny bird fallen from the eaves, waiting with wide
eyes for whatever would sniff it out.

"What are you thinking?" Linda asked.

"Not a lot. What about you?"

"I was thinking of a character in a book who looked
at a chestnut tree so hard, he couldn't remember its
name. That's what happens to me here. I look out at the
flatness, and I'm swallowed up in it. I forget who I am.
God, if I had to live on the farm again, I'd lose my
mind."

Ellen smiled toward the tree in reassurance. Oak. How
could anyone forget the name? "He must have been
crazy."

"No, just French."

"Doesn't surprise me."

The girl let out a loud, raspy guffaw that startled her
mother. Since she'd risen to whatever she'd risen to,
Linda smiled a lot, but she didn't laugh much. Ellen
watched her run a finger along the curve of her short
black hair, the way women did on TV when they were
nervous, and wondered at the contradiction.

"Isn't it strange?" Linda cried delightedly, as though

strangeness pleased her. "I love you more than anyone I know, but I look at you and you look at me, and we might as well be glass. Zip! Right through."

Her mother studied the oak. Abrupt confessions were another part of the new personality, but Ellen rather resented them, even when they appeared as declarations of love. She thought, irrelevantly, of how many colors there were in what people called brown.

"Is there someone who can see into you, Lin?" she asked, hoping there might be a man somewhere she'd told only her father about.

But just then Peggy returned and stood above her, stretching her back, her hands on either side of her belly as if she were adjusting the load. She was five months along and already beginning to feel the ache. "Out like a light—about time, too. Where'd Dad go?"

Deborah was right behind her. "Ellen, will you settle an argument? How many minutes a pound is it for turkey —fifteen or twenty? The thermometer's . . . I don't know what's wrong with it."

To answer, she had to lean around Peggy, who was straddling her to get down into the yard. "It depends. Twenty, I think. Maybe longer when it's stuffed. It's been so long since I've used the oven for meat."

Peggy hallooed. Linda stood and brushed off her pants. "Gordon's here."

As the blue van crackled into the lane, Deborah wrung her hands of the turkey and of her sister-in-law with the microwave. "I guess it doesn't make that much difference."

Ellen waved to her son without getting up. The four children who were Gordon and Myra's had sped to the fence and were shaking it with the weight of their accumulated grievances even before their parents had climbed out of the van. Gordon in his business suit and Myra carrying a grocery bag strode across the yard in

procession, talking half to their kids, half to their relatives on the porch.

"About time!" Billy Nafziger called down. "Goddamned Bears are in it: 10–7."

"You should have seen the mess," Gordon said. "Josh,
shut up! I'm lucky I didn't have to eat out of the vending
machines."

"What are they doing, working you on Thanksgiving?"

"Computers," Gordon complained. "They're worse
than milk cows."

Then why didn't you stay on the farm the way your
father wanted? Ellen thought as he kissed her on the
cheek, leaving behind the stink of soap and after-shave.
He hugged Linda off her feet, and the two of them, arm
in arm, trooped into the house, followed by the rest of
the procession, Myra bringing up the rear, listening to
Josh.

"It hurt! It hurt, Ma!"

"It couldn't have hurt that much. You're still walking."

The children were instantly outside again, jumping
over her into the yard as if she were an obstacle in a
game. I should go in, Ellen told herself, but made no
move. It would mean getting dizzy when she stood up,
listening to more old gossip or watching football, which
she loathed—too much effort when all a woman really
wanted to do was lie in the sun and doze. Head back, the
sun on her face, she gazed across the fields into the offing,
but she couldn't find any comfort in it. She wished Linda
had answered her question.

Helmets in hands, the Detroit players filed back onto the
playing field, while a blond TV star sang "America the
Beautiful" as if she were blind drunk in the back of a
pickup truck, Marion thought.

"Any of that cheese left?" he asked his father.

Walter Elder lay back in the La-Z-Boy and contentedly squashed a hunk of cheese between two crackers. "No, all gone."

The first-half stats appeared over a shot of the Detroit cheerleaders doing splits in unison.

"Oooo-ee, look at them," Dwight Cooper chortled.

"Three turnovers," Gordon moaned, throwing his coat over the back of a folding chair. "No wonder we're behind."

From the floor Billy squinted up at the screen. "What do they do to make their tits push up like that?"

"Socks."

"C'mon, Dwight."

"Socks, I swear to God, they put them in . . . underneath. Remember Pam Davis, Marion? Used to run around with Beth in high school. Make a pass, and you'd end up with a handful of argyle."

From the Goodyear blimp, they saw downtown Detroit, the river, the Silverdome; then the picture switched to the playing field, where the players were stretching and the cheerleaders high-kicking in chorus.

"Whatever happened to Pam?" Gordon asked.

Billy Nafziger lay back, hands behind his neck, and laughed. "Took up with a saxophone player from Peoria."

"Black?"

"As the ace of spades."

"I'll be damned."

Marion leaned forward and peeked into the cheese jar just to be sure, took a couple of crackers, and settled back.

Walter Elder, peering at the screen over his belly, let out a ponderous sigh. "Don't look like socks to me."

All of them heard a car pull up and the door slam. They smiled at one another and resettled themselves so they could see. The children outside shouted. Arthur could be heard on the porch talking to his wife. Four-year-old

Ginny Frisch appeared on the other side of the screen door and laboriously pried it open.

"Thank you, sweetheart," Arthur said as he sidled through. "Grandpa will come back in a minute and give you a kiss."

Then with a whoop, he burst into the room.

"Ye are saved!" He held out a large cardboard box with the words *Altar Candles* marked on the side. "Your friends and neighbors, hearing that evil times had fallen upon you, gave what little they could so that not one of us should go thirsty." Kneeling, he overturned the box. Cans and bottles of beer in every color, shape, and size tumbled onto the rug. "I've got Miller, Pabst, Budweiser, Schlitz—you name it, I've got it. Walter?"

Marion's father poked through the colorful rubble. "Schlitz, thank you."

"Billy, you want a Bud?"

"Maybe. What's the green one?"

"Arthur, what have you done?"

Deborah stood above him, hands on hips, her mouth trembling between smile and scream. The women came out of the kitchen to watch.

"Looky here, two bottles of Anchor steam beer from Reverend Laesch. You ought to keep an eye on that man, sister."

For a moment, the smile won out. "Where on earth did you get all these?"

Arthur sat on his heels and proceeded to count them on his fingers. "Let's see, there was the Ambergs, Ottos, Watkins, Harpers, Shoemakers, Stahleys, Rupps, Amberg finally put a lightning rod on his barn, now that the season's over. And Reverend Laesch—let's not forget him."

By the end of the list, her expression had depreciated into the small, resigned grimace of a girl whose brother cannot be reasoned with.

"You don't need to humiliate me."

"Humiliate you?" Arthur was in no mood to relent. "I didn't say a damned thing about you. I said, 'We ran out of beer.' Here, Chuck, try some of this."

"You're not giving that boy a beer!"

"Sure looks like I am."

"Chuck . . . "

A white plume of foam gushed from the boy's can, spattering the coffee table, the TV, and his cousin Gordon, while on the screen Chicago's return specialist fielded the kickoff and was instantly buried under a pile of blue-and-silver jerseys.

Deborah exploded. "Jesus Christ!"

"Listen to her. Marion, didn't you ever teach that boy how to open a beer? Tap the top, boy. Tap the top."

Gordon laughed as he swiped at his pants. The men were laughing; the women laughed in the doorway to the kitchen. And Chuckie, red from ear to ear, made furious stabs at the big puddle on the coffee table with a cocktail napkin. Beth came running in with a sponge and a roll of towels, but by that time most of what had been on the table was on the floor.

Deborah flared at her brother. "This is your fault, and it's not funny!"

"My fault I had to drive gravel roads with a boxful of beer? Hell, Deb, I'm contributing to the boy's education. How's he ever going to get laid if he can't open a beer?"

Slowly, deliberately, she breathed herself into the possession by which she had withstood him for nearly fifty years. She asked Marion if he would see to it that the mess was cleaned up and returned to the kitchen, as if there were no one she knew in the room and the accident had happened twenty years ago.

Marion set his mangled cigar aside and pushed himself up in the chair till he was eye to eye with his brother-in-law. "You know, sometimes I wish the two of you could have gotten married. It would have saved the rest of us a whole hell of a lot of grief."

The same saving faculty that had allowed Deborah to imagine her son innocently sipping Cokes with a sexless gang of friends led her to the notion that Arthur had made a fool of himself. It was, after all, her Thanksgiving. The family had come to her house, their children were playing in her yard, they would sit at her table, and through the agency of her husband, she would serve them. This was not simply an idea to her; it was an emotion, like honor. On this day, in this place, they were hers as much as the child who once kicked in her womb. She might not care for these women or their men, but in giving them cheese and crackers and inviting them to her table, she felt a love as genuine as the words she spoke to God. She treated the turkey as if it were a land claim (only she could baste), and she had to be the one to assign jobs to the others (would Beth please peel the potatoes?), not out of pride, but out of a possessive kind of love.

Soon after she had finished with Arthur, she had Grandma moved out of the kitchen, where she was too much in the way. Sink, counter, and kitchen table became workstations for potato peeling, bean cutting, salad making, and so on, and the women who had jobs defended themselves against the encroachment of help from those who did not. Beth was not imposed upon, there being only one peeler; but Peggy, at the table with bowls and two heads of lettuce, soon found herself foreman of a tomato slicer, a celery chopper, and a carver of rosettes out of radishes. Linda was allowed to make a vinaigrette, there being plenty of good bottled dressing available. Once she'd ordered the preparations to her satisfaction, Deborah took another poke at the turkey with the meat fork and saw no red in the juice. According to the fifteen-minute schedule, it should be done, but if she let it roast until after the football game, she would be certain.

Now she remembered that she had wanted Chuck to set up the card tables and chairs on the porch for the children, but rather than confront him again, she did it herself. The moment she began, the children rushed up, seemingly out of nowhere, and left just as quickly, whining and griping, when they discovered that dinner wasn't ready. Granny must have discovered there was a game on TV because when Deborah eavesdropped on the living room she could hear the old woman pestering Arthur for details.

"What's happening? Why can't they stop him?"

And Arthur, whose patience had always amazed his sister, shouted back outrageous capsules of the action.

As it turned out, the game dragged on for over an hour. The Bears lost, but not badly, and the men came away from the TV talking quarterbacks. The big silver platter, etched in oak leaves, was carried in from the breakfront. Green beans were set to steam, potato mashers were mobilized, flour was requisitioned from the pantry, and the men were forced bodily from the room while Deborah and Beth lifted the turkey in its pan to the counter.

The smell of sage and thyme filled the air. The huge golden bird rested high on its palanquin like a beautiful promise. The women ooed, the dispossessed men cried, "Something smells good in there," and the children could not be kept out. With a scraping of chairs, the men began to seat themselves at the table. In the midst of the commotion, Deborah moved happily, feeling generous and complete and loved.

Ellen handed her the meat fork, and Deborah forced it down next to the breastbone. The liquid that drained out was clear as water. Holding the neck down to keep the stuffing from coming out, she and Ellen carefully lifted the bird onto its silver platter so that her mother-in-law

could make a roux. In the transfer, however, the fork-
marks bled, this time a brilliant pink. No one else noticed,
and for an instant Deborah considered trying to hide the
fact, but when Martha Elder dipped a spoon into the
flour, she stopped her and asked Ellen to get a knife.

Even then, few noticed what was going on, until Marion
complained, "You're not going to carve that bird, are
you?"

"Go to hell!" she snapped.

Everyone was quiet.

Three cuts, and each told the same story. At the surface
and most of the way down, the meat was done, but it was
pink farther in. She threw the carving knife into the sink
and stood back, wiping her hands over and over on her
apron while Ellen and Beth returned the turkey to the
pan.

Some wanted to eat it anyway. They were silenced,
along with those who said, We might at least have the
salad. The turkey went back into the oven at a higher
temperature, the mashed potatoes were covered, and it
was decided to make a casserole out of the beans. The
children were inconsolable. They mobbed together
around the dining room table, scavenging the relish
dishes and grieving over the lost turkey as if it had been
stolen from them; finally they had to be put down by
violence, and even then it was only the promise of sandwiches that kept them contained.

Since something had to be held responsible, the
women blamed the thermometer, the cookbooks, the gro-
cer, and the bird itself. It was as close as they could come
to exonerating Deborah. But she stood aside, listening to
their well-meaning justifications with a slight, satiric
smile and wondering seriously if God might not have intended this to chasten her pride. In her world, accidents
and miscalculations did not exist. Even a rock in her shoe
was a sign, and all signs were from God, so that even pain

expressed the mystery of a greater purpose—and so her
relatives' excuses seemed petty-minded. The fault was
hers. Why did they want to take it away from her?

When Myra and Linda took peanut-butter-and-jelly
sandwiches out to the kids, Deborah followed as far as
the screen door. Around the oak in the middle of the
yard, Peggy and Billy had started a ring game with the
younger kids, singing, "Ring a ring a rosy, pocket full of
posies . . . " Marion, with some of the other men, their
shirtsleeves up, peered under the hood of his pickup. Art
snored on the couch, and Grandma Frisch nodded in her
chair nearby. "Ashes, ashes, all fall down!" For a while
Deborah pondered the fields, which seemed to reel
uneasily toward the horizon, attending to the voices in
silence. Then she took off her apron, laying it over a chair,
and walked down the narrow central hallway to her bedroom, closed the door gently behind her, and didn't come
out again for half an hour.

Once more, the potatoes were warmed with hot milk.
The casserole was wedged in, the turkey probed and dis-
cussed, and this time Deborah let the others do the work,
afraid to touch anything lest it, too, turn out wrong. The
women continued to offer their spurious consolations.
The only one who seemed to understand was Ellen, who
simply embraced her and said nothing. Deborah held her
sister-in-law's hand in both of hers and felt comforted for
a moment before she considered whose comfort she was
taking.

Several of the women wondered if, when the meal was
finally served, she would sit at the table or retreat into
the bedroom again. They knew she was the kind of person who fell apart when things didn't go her way. But
after the kids had been shooed to the porch, their paper
plates piled with food, and after the adults had settled

once more into whatever places suited them—grease
under their fingernails and moons of sweat under their
arms, carrying the irritated expressions of people resigned to their duty—Deborah stood behind her chair at
the foot of the table and said, "Let us pray."

Looking straight before her, over Marion's bowed head
to the empty shelf on the breakfront where the silver tray
had been displayed, she spoke in a voice other than her
own—rounder and more vibrant—in a poetry she herself
would have thought extravagant if it had been addressed
to anyone but God, yet simple and direct, as though God
were a man she was reminding of His responsibilities.

"Our Heavenly Father, You who gave us life and the
bounty of the earth to sustain life, we praise You. We
thank You for all the goodness in our lives. Give us not
just our daily bread, but the bread of Your body, which is
everlasting life. Blind us with Your love so that we may
see, deafen us with Your voice so that we may hear, and
bind us to Your will so that we may find freedom. If we
don't understand Your ways, if we are proud and foolish
and put our hope in vain things, give us to know our
mistakes and to love the Truth when we see it. Purify our
minds from the dark thoughts that tie our souls to earth.
O Lord, we would have them fly to Your mercy seat, as
pure and light as the driven snow."

Chuck was hateful, and, worse, he liked being hateful.
It felt good. He was trying not to give in, but it was as if
God couldn't stop telling him how disgusting he was. For
the feeling in his mother's words seemed to overwhelm
their meaning, just as the warmth of his secret dreams
melted his best intentions.

*Her fingertips brushed lightly along the curve of his
chin, down the vee of his neck, until one finger hooked
over the top button of his shirt.*

"Soon" she said. "I promise."

"We know we are weak and undeserving. We have

denied You. Because we did not trust in You, we looked
into the valley of the shadow and cried, 'Any way but that
way, Lord!' We have complicated our lives with dreams
and imaginings till we can no longer see You, were You
to stand before us in all Your glory. But through Your
Son, Jesus, who shed His blood that we might be reborn,
who died and rose again in the flesh on the third day, that
we might see You in Your majesty, make us like little
children in our belief. Forgive us and bring us the joy of
Your Holy Spirit."

*The finger dropped from its roost and landed a couple
of buttons down.*

"Why not now?"

*"Because. Oh, Chuck, you're so dense! Is that all you
care about—getting some? I don't want my cherry
busted, I want to be happy. I want to feel beautiful."*

*"You are beautiful." He was going to add, "And I love
you," but he was afraid.*

*Her hand fell again, and, startled, he glanced down to
be sure of what he'd felt.*

*"Did I hurt you?" She'd barely touched him, but from
the concern in her voice, she must have felt that the
slightest pressure would give him pain.*

"No, feels fine."

*"You sure?" She probed the outline of his penis as if
she were exploring a welt.*

"Feels great."

*Her fingers circled round and round the zipper of his
jeans, then lifted and unhooked the clasp of his belt.*

"I really do love you."

"Release us from our burden of sin that we may sing
Your praises. We praise You for the good earth, for the
rain and the sun and the beauty of this harvest season.
We thank You for our health, for our homes and families;
we thank You for our neighbors and friends and for the
freedom to speak and worship as we please. We thank

You for the hope and truth and beauty in all things, no
matter how frail or misguided, that serve the Lord. But
most of all we thank You for the promise that one day we
will leave this earthly prison and be lifted up to glory."

*Holly leaned across him, nestling against his left arm
as if she didn't want him to see what she was doing. He
could feel her laughing as she tried to pull the elastic of
his shorts over his hard-on. "You need a hinge." Finally,
she drew it out through the placket. He stroked her hair,
feeling cut off and lonely with her back to him, even as he
was slouching in the seat to give her more room. He
pulled the back of her blouse from her jeans, so at least
he could touch her skin, kissed a vertebra, and frowned.*

"It doesn't make sense to me."

Deborah confronted the rows of more or less bent
heads defiantly. "We thank You for this meal, and for all
Your gifts to us."

"Poor Chuckie," Holly giggled.

"And may each of us accomplish Your will in all we do,
for we pray in the name of Jesus Christ, our Lord."

"Poor poor Chuckie."

"Amen."

Everyone turned toward Marion except Chuck, who
drooped in his chair looking half-drowned. "Chuck,"
Deborah mourned in her own voice again, "it would be
nice if, just once, you could sit up like a human being."

The plates had been gathered and stacked at the head of
the table, the food set on a card table to Marion's right.
As his wife shook her cloth napkin open, he rose, knife in
hand, and plunged the meat fork into the turkey.

"White meat, Ma?"

Martha nodded.

"Gravy on your dressing? Cranberry sauce? Beans?"

He served them, though it would have been easier to

pass around the food, and he served them by precedence, though they sat in no order. It was the ritual of the day, a bit more formality than usual—manners brought out like the silver for special occasions, but no less genuine for their rarity.

The rolls made their way around the table, followed at a respectful distance by the butter and preserves. Salads had already been put at each place, every one with its democratic allotment of two tomato wedges, two black olives, and a radish rose.

"Ellen?" Marion had to raise his voice to be heard at the other end of the table, where she was feeding Grandma Frisch. The old woman was staring straight ahead and eating mechanically as if she didn't want to be associated with what her mouth was doing.

"Dark, Marion. And just a little gravy on the potatoes."

It was time for the food to be praised, but no one knew what to say. Compliments were tried, but Deborah kept her eyes on her husband and did not respond.

Walter Elder mentioned that the John Deere dealer in Lexington had gone under, but that didn't carry the conversation very far.

"Here you are, Beth. Myra, white or dark? Go ahead, girls. Don't wait on the rest of us."

"Some of both, if you don't mind."

Taking her plate, Beth observed that Penney's in the Eastland Mall was having a white sale tomorrow. If she went, she was going without him, Dwight said. Ellen remembered that she needed new towels, the green ones were getting raggy. Marion's mother vowed she wouldn't go within ten miles of the mall the day after Thanksgiving.

"Here's yours, Peg. With some extra for the passenger. Linda?"

"Chuck's not doing anything tomorrow," Deborah said to Beth. "He'd be glad to drive you."

From the widespread animation that greeted her offer,

one would have thought that they all had errands for
Chuck to run.

Ellen passed up the line the dessert plate she'd been
using for Granny's food. "Put a little white meat on that,
would you, please? Very thin."

"Will do. Dad?"

Gordon asked Chuck what colleges he was considering.
Even at that simple question, the boy hummed and
blushed and made strange gestures with the handle of his
fork. Finally, he admitted that the coach at Illinois State
had sort of offered him a baseball scholarship if he
pitched well this spring, but it was still up in the air. Then
he glanced at his father to see if he'd said anything wrong.

"Enough gravy for you, Arthur? Now, as I remember,
Gordy, you're a leg man." Marion added that if the boy
got accepted to a good college out of state, he could probably find the money to send him.

Martha Elder choked on a piece of meat and had to
have her back slapped.

Deborah wanted to know when he had decided that,
but her husband deflected the question by saying something vague about Chuck being on his own and making
new friends.

"He's got more friends than he knows what to do with,"
she complained. "He doesn't need to go halfway across
the country to find friends."

While Marion heaped a plate for his son, Billy Nafziger
complained that the damned bank computer had nearly
cost him his FHA loan.

"Grandpa." There was a scratching on the screen door.

Had Chuck thought about computers? Gordon wanted
to know. Chuck hadn't. Well, if he did, Gordon knew a
man at Baylor and another man at Ohio State and another at UCLA, and all of them knew other men. Chuck
should think about it. Computers were the name of the
game.

"Grandpa!"

Arthur tried to look around Walter Elder but gave it up and asked his daughter-in-law. "Is that who I think it is?"

Myra nodded. "Notice who she's not talking to."

"There's a farm sale at John Kinsinger's next month," Dwight said. "The FHA dumped him."

"What do you want, Ginny?" Arthur asked.

But it was Josh who answered. "We're done. Can we have dessert?" A scattershot chorus of children's voices agreed that they wanted dessert, that they'd been waiting forever.

"You eat your green beans?"

Two voices cried, "Yes." Josh complained that there was stuff in them that tasted like onions.

Seeing Peggy arch her shoulders, Deborah asked, "Back hurt?"

"Always does, but with Artie it didn't start so soon."

"Go back and eat your green beans, and we'll get you some pumpkin pie," Arthur instructed.

The chorus tried to complain, but Myra cut them off. "I want you all to go sit quietly at your tables until we're finished, or you won't get a damned thing! You hear?" She ducked her head like a conspirator to hide her laughter. "That'll shut them up."

"You should see a chiropractor. I've been going to Dr. Powell for the last . . . oh, it must be ten years now, and he's done wonders for me."

Beth had stopped eating. She laid her hand lightly over Dwight's and frowned at a pop-up crepe turkey. It was rough, she said, to sell off everything just before Christmas.

"Grandpa!" Ginny stood inside the front door, just out of range of the nearest adult arm—a thin girl with a narrow face hedged by dark curls.

"Yes, sweetheart?"

"I don't like pupkin pie."

Myra pointed her fork in the direction of the screen.
"There's ice cream and chocolate sauce in the fridge. If
you want a sundae, you'd better get yourself back on the
porch."

"I don't feel sorry for Kinsinger," Gordon declared.
"He knew the risks. He took his chances, and he lost.
That's life—survival of the fittest."

Peggy didn't want a chiropractor poking at her while
she was pregnant, she said, but her aunt wouldn't hear of
such nonsense.

"Don't listen to the doctors," Deborah pleaded.
"They're only protecting their pocketbooks. Try him. You
won't regret it, I promise."

There were several chunks of meat stacked on the fork
Billy Nafziger was pointing at Gordon. Billy liked his meat
in small bites, but he ate three or four at a time. "You
mean if I take this fork and shove it upside your Adam's
apple, I'm the fittest?"

"If I can't defend myself."

"That's not how it works," Linda said softly in a tone
that made both men busy themselves with their food.

His plate empty in front of him, Marion was already
offering seconds, and there were plenty of takers. Old ate
faster than young, country ate faster than city, so that
Walter Elder had finished two helpings and was contentedly sopping rolls into the pool of gravy on his plate while
Linda had yet to finish her salad, which for some reason
she had saved for last. When Marion finally stopped serv-
ing, Myra and Deb were already on the porch stuffing
paper plates into a garbage bag and taking dessert orders. The moment he sat, what was left of the dinner
etiquette dissolved. The women began to clear the table,
and Marion became nothing more than what he was, a
man chewing on the thighbone of a turkey.

Martha Elder and her daughter set out coffee cups and
ashtrays. Linda tried to help, but her hand was captured

by Walter, who had something more to tell her about a girl he'd known in 1937. Myra went out the door butt first with a tray of pie slices and an aerosol can of whipped cream, followed by Deborah with ice-cream sundaes. Ellen brushed scraps of turkey from Granny's dress. And Chuck, thinking sourly that, by now, he should be at a friend's house shooting baskets, tossed a wax pilgrim from one hand to the other while his uncle Arthur lectured him about hogs. The questions that had come from the head of the table were now shouted out from the kitchen—mince, apple, or pumpkin? A la mode? Cheese? Whipped cream?

Peggy returned with a sleep-red baby Arthur in her arms, who for a minute or two stared at the confusion around him in openmouthed fascination, then buried his face between his mother's breasts and howled.

No one noticed Granny uncurl herself, or her hand steal from cup to plate to candle, or how she bit down on her tongue in concentration. No one noticed until an empty water glass escaped her and tumbled to the floor.

"What's up, babe?" Arthur shouted.

Her hand stayed on the table, and her face took on an expression that was something like vanity.

She said, "Hot fudge."

Ellen came out from the kitchen and seeing the set jaw asked, "What does she want?"

"I'm not sure. . . ." Arthur shrugged.

But then Granny interrupted him, addressing a spot where the sun glowed on the table. "I want a hot-fudge sundae."

Ellen threw up her hands. "Oh, God."

There was nothing she could do about that. Ellen squeezed the old woman's shoulder and went back to the kitchen; Deborah emerged a moment later carrying slabs of pie.

"Here you are, Walter, Chuck."

Bending down, she took her grandmother's hands in hers. "Don't you remember what the doctor said? Sugar is bad for you. Sugar could kill you. You wouldn't want that, would you?" She pressed the old woman's hands onto her lap as if she were pressing a tack into the wall.

"Isn't there some substitute?" Walter asked.

"She won't touch them. Says she can tell the difference." With one hand Deborah picked up Chuck's plate, with the other she squeezed the thick muscle at the base of his neck. "She's a child. She wants what she wants when she wants it, and if you don't give in, she pouts."

"So you get your revenge talking about her like she's not here," Chuck responded, and the men stared at him.

"She doesn't know what we're talking about," Deborah said.

"I'll bet."

It was Arthur who came to his sister's defense. "Can't hear worth shit. I turn on the radio, give her the headphones, and she's got to have it all the way up—eight, nine, ten—before she can hear anything. Christ, I'm surprised she's got eardrums left."

"Then how does she know we have sundaes?"

"Smells them. Hey, don't laugh, boy. That old wreck's got a nose like a bloodhound." Arthur tapped his own considerable nose.

Chuck snorted his disbelief, but the rest looked down the table at the old woman, who glared back at them—or so it seemed—with eyes that swam in the thickness of her glasses, hands tugging at her dress as if she were testing rope.

But there was nothing they could do for her, and there were other things to talk about, pie to eat and coffee to drink, and some of the children were already whining to go home, so they left her alone. They hadn't seen that she'd been active all dinner long, hurrying more rolls into the oven, shooing children from the icebox, teasing a man dead thirty years that he was getting fat; they couldn't know with what rage she murmured to herself, imprisoned in this senseless shell, until she began to wad up the edge of the tablecloth.

When Ellen touched her, she shied away.

"No!" she cried, and stood, clutching the cloth to her breast. "Leave me alone. I hate you! You want me dead!" she screamed, staggering backward, dragging the dishes with her, as everyone sat stunned. "I hate you!" Then she fell, and the whole Thanksgiving table—pie plates, coffee cups, ashtrays, candles, pinecones—followed her to the floor.

They steeled themselves for the cry of pain, for the ambulance and the dying, but there was no cry. When Deborah knelt beside her, she found her unhurt, curled like a baby on the rug, rubbing the cloth against her cheek as if she couldn't get enough of its softness.

I I I

ARTHUR had to accept that there was no other choice but to send his grandmother where she could be properly cared for. Even so, what convinced him was not the weight of the argument, but the fact that his wife had agreed. Bewildered and hurt, unable to comprehend the anger of a woman to whom she'd given so much, Ellen had simply stopped caring. When the family met soon after Thanksgiving, she was forced to confess this to him, and Arthur wept. Tears would not have been necessary, Marion reminded him, if he had listened to them in the first place.

Granny had to be told, of course. Since Arthur couldn't

bring himself to do it, his wife tried to break the news, but the old woman ignored her. Arthur finally had to confront her, while the family looked on from the kitchen. Granny whimpered and begged, she tried to apologize, but he was not the same man. When she finally realized no argument would save her, she barricaded herself in the downstairs bedroom, declaring that this was her house and she'd die in it.

From that point on, she couldn't be left alone, even when she went to the bathroom. Relatives and friends were enlisted to sit with her, and this had the effect of confusing her still more. She began to lose her grasp of names and times and places and often thought that she had already been, as she called it, "committed."

Occasionally, there were lapses. Ellen returned from the barn one day to find water boiling on the stove, and later a highway patrolman showed up at the door, investigating a report that an elderly woman had been bound to a chair by thieves.

Deborah had researched institutions some time ago, so the family was able to settle fairly quickly on a small Methodist nursing home outside Congerville. They were told to expect a wait of several months, but before the week was out the director had called back to say they could take her in January. Granny accepted the news calmly, asking only if they'd let her listen to the radio. However, twice since then she'd been caught trying to maneuver her walker through the snow—on her way to Texas, she claimed. No one was amused.

Someone suggested celebrating Christmas in her honor, but that was a cousin who hadn't been to dinner on Thanksgiving. Arthur commissioned a carpenter friend to sculpt a wooden relief of her and Charlie from a World War I–vintage snapshot she had on the dresser upstairs. People spoke openly of her expenses and of the fairest way to divvy up her possessions.

The greatest surprise during the last month had been the friendship, of sorts, that had sprung up between Grandma and Chuck. It appeared to revolve mostly around sports and the nice girl who called her "Nana." Even Chuck didn't know what to make of it.

Four days before Christmas, Grandma Frisch sat in an easy chair near the stereo, her Chicago Cubs cap on, listening to a basketball tournament through the headphones. Ellen and Arthur had gone shopping at the mall. The room was dark, except for the light from the Christmas tree near the window and the blue glow from the receiver's dial, and Chuck was depressed.

He and Holly had been lying together on the couch, their shoes off, talking about friends and basketball and the old woman in the easy chair, as if they mattered. But to Chuck everything seemed flat and false. Nothing mattered. He loved no one. The earth could have opened and swallowed everyone on it, including Holly, and he wouldn't have batted an eye. Now and then they'd embrace and kiss—deep, long kisses full of energy but without much feeling—and she would rub against him until his prick got hard, yet he felt no more passion than an amputee at the bending of his mechanical arm. Every object in the room was as far from him as the nearest star, and that distance was as solid as a wall. There were walls around the couch, and walls around the walls, and he'd be stuck playing this phony game forever. The distances inside himself were just as great, and every time she touched him they grew.

He wondered if this were the punishment for being a fake—that you only got a make-believe version of what you wanted. If he'd simply and honestly loved some nice, simple girl, maybe he'd have gotten laid by now. But his emotions never worked that way. They were full of self-

ishness and craft, of complications—in a word, of sin—
even from the start. Last summer, when he'd first gone
out with her, it was because his friends said she was easy,
and he was shy. He'd secreted a rubber in the pocket of
his billfold where credit cards were supposed to go. It
was still there, reminding him. Oddly enough, he continued to think of her as easy, but he liked her, too, and now
he had come to depend on her. After all, she was smart
and easygoing and a lot of things he wasn't. She knew
how to handle people and made him laugh at himself. It
felt weird, this in-betweenness, and he suspected it must
be unusual because there were no words to describe it:
"lust" was too crude and "love" was too spiritual, and
imagining anything half and half was like planting corn in
quicksand. When the complications got him down, an
emptiness would rise up inside him and separate the
pieces as though there were a thousand miles between
them.

In the darkness he could feel her frizzy black hair
crushed against his arm, which comforted him a little.
Again, he drew her close, hoping she might protect him
from himself, but the dark smell of her hair made him
lonely.

"What's the matter, Chuck?"

"Nothing. I'm tired."

"You shouldn't practice so hard." She kissed his neck
and, hugging him as tightly as she could, marveled at the
power of her body.

She didn't have to do a thing, it was just there—with
him, his friends, her mother's boyfriends. Holly liked her
power, liked thinking she could wound or heal at will,
liked to believe that she was the agent of great forces; but
the idea made her uneasy, too. She couldn't make herself
invisible, turn the power off, or forget it.

She let go of him and lay back, wondering if he were
bored. She despised his impatience. Sooner or later they

would sneak past Granny, go into the back bedroom and shut the door, and she'd let him come in her hand. Till then there was this lovely not-quiteness, kissing and fondling with their clothes on, feeling sex all over them like a blush. Sometimes she wondered why people bothered going farther, when you could float like this forever and make your feeling into whatever you wanted.

But she had loved Chuck, almost from the first, for the very things that annoyed her: his silences, his hopes and doubts and the fact that he was, in a nice sort of way, dull, and his bizarre points of honor. By sixteen she had known more boys than she'd wanted to, but Chuck was the first to come up with the word *honor.* She thought it was cute.

She loved him because it was fated, and fate knew what was best for her. About God she had many doubts, but fate she believed in absolutely. No universe, she was sure, would be so cruel as to not care about her happiness, so all she had to do was follow the signs and the right doors would open, the wrong ones close. The whole art of life lay in recognizing the inevitable. That was why she did so well in school—she assumed the right answer would come, and it usually did. Even when she got hurt, she'd look back and realize the hurt had been necessary. Because her father had run off, her mother had taken her out of Catholic school. Because their neighbor had been robbed and raped, they had moved to the country. Because the farm girls sneered at her, she had taken to sunning herself on the raft anchored in the middle of Miller's Pond, where a boy, with yellow hair and eyes so blue you wanted to swim in them, had borrowed her lotion.

If it wasn't fate, why would she have fallen in love with someone so unlike her expectations? Even if, in the end, Chuck didn't turn out to be the right guy, she was sure he was the right direction. She dreamed of a home and a husband and lots of kids, somewhere away from people

who knew everything—where, if her mother came to the
door, she wouldn't have to answer. But whether the
dream came true was for fate to decide.

"You want to go in the other room?" she sighed.

"No," he said sharply, putting her in her place.

The bastard. God, he was weird. Sensitive and incredi-
bly dense, gentle and brutal all at once, staring off into
space as if he were thinking about someone else. There
were times when she felt nostalgic for the blunt-spoken
guys in her old neighborhood, until she saw them reflected in her mother's latest boyfriend.

Her mother's boyfriends, that long line of men with
different faces but the same smirk. Men who knew everything and made jokes about it. Men who, like her mother,
bragged about all that they didn't like or want or believe,
who looked at her, sprawled in front of the television,
like something hanging on a hook behind the drug
counter. Her mother hated them and would tell Holly the
intimate details of their failures, and Holly assumed she
told them stories about her, too.

Feeling a bit bored herself, she glanced past her feet
toward Nana Frisch in her chair.

"I love that cap."

"Yeah, isn't it crazy?" Chuck said. "I brought it back
for Uncle Art, but he gave it to her. She thinks it brings
her teams luck."

"The Cubs?"

"That's what she thinks."

"Normal cuts it to eight. Jeff Blumgarten in at center for
Springfield-Griffin. Cooper brings the ball up court under
pressure from Stahley. Normal now comes out man to
man. Cooper passes to Caspar Williams, to his brother
Jimmy, back to Cas. Cas dribbles across the key, goes up
behind Blumgarten's pick . . . No! Fakes the shot, passes

to Blumgarten rolling to the hoop. Two! A perfect pick and roll, and Griffin is back up by ten. Boy, that was pretty!"

She could hear the crowd's cheers, but they had no hold on her; she could see the pass loop over the stunned defense, but it was like a reflection on a window while outside terrible things were happening. Since they'd taken her future from her, the past would not obey. Memories stumbled over one another, names and places disappeared, and without them what she remembered was as hazy as what she could see with her own eyes.

Beneath the shadows was a single dark object she knew must be death. But death was none of her business. Her business was to fight back. She looked for her guards —the boy who dropped things and the girl who smelled of mushrooms and hay—where the gloom was the darkest. Nothing moved. Even these children were her enemies.

Thanksgiving had given her anger—not against this one or that one, but against them all. They were thieves. She had trusted them, and they had betrayed her. Because they claimed to love her, she'd gone along when they handed her a cane, and when they said, "Don't eat this. Don't eat that." Then slowly, as if it wasn't their fault but hers, they'd stolen the sound of the leaves and they'd taken the fields that stretched out for miles—so that her mind wandered in silence like a lonely dog. When she had rebelled, they'd said she was being silly, and she'd caved in. That was how they controlled you, they made you stop being silly.

She didn't remember or care about the details of what she'd done at the dinner. What had infuriated her, finally, was not the food or the people, but the sudden revelation that the tablecloth between her fingers was hers—her favorite, the one her sister had ordered from Passau and had given to her and Charlie, a month late, for their anniversary. She could not recall her sister's last name, but she knew exactly where the tablecloth ought to have been stored. No one had asked her permission—they had just taken it, the way they'd taken everything else she loved.

"Time out. A minute to go in the half and Normal down by twelve."

She wished somebody would turn off the damned radio, but she was afraid if she asked, they might not ever turn it back on again.

"Arthur!" she cried in exasperation.

The shadows became fluid, a light went on, and she smelled hay. The earphones were lifted off. The boy asked, "What do you want, Grandma?"

"I'm cold."

Albert Meyers had brought in the biggest harvest that year, so the dance was his responsibility. He had set a bonfire in the yard between the outbuildings and put out bales of straw for people to sit on. She and her sister had arrived late deliberately. Their neighbors had made a cir- cle around the fire and were dancing the polka to Paul Kammerer's accordion. Her sister drank cider, and then they took a turn around the fire, stopping here and there to talk to friends. She nearly broke into tears thinking Charlie hadn't come, but when they returned to the cider table, there he was—had been there, in fact, all along— straddling a bale and watching her. She could have gladly murdered him. She hated the way he stared at her, hated the way he sat on the bale, hated him for not letting her know he was there. He stood up and wiped his hands on his pants as if he were about to chop some wood. As he came closer, his body threw a shadow across her. There were witty remarks she had practiced, and cutting things she wanted to say, but when she saw that he wasn't smil- ing, she bowed her head in shame. Only for a second. When she looked up, her face was bright with triumph.

Still, he wouldn't acknowledge it.

She reached out, slyly, and hooked one finger into the pocket of his shirt. She said, "Shoes."

Try as he might, he couldn't hold himself back any longer. He pawed the ground like a horse, and his laugh —his big, loud laugh—made people turn. "*Ja.* Shoes."

Then he took her hand and led her toward the fire.

The shawl interrupted her memory, and the girl's hand on her cheek brought her back. For a moment, she contemplated her own strangeness. The woman who danced, the woman who had crocheted this shawl, so many women—they all still lived as long as she did not try to stand. She reached out in the direction of the lamp.

"Honey."

The girl stepped across the light and took her hand.

"I made this." She brought the girl's hand to the cloth.

"It's lovely, Nana."

The shawl was ratty and faded and probably hadn't been very pretty when it was new, but as Holly let the woman's cold hand guide her own, what she felt was envy.

"Took me six months. Six months! Always somebody barging in. Always some damned fool thing to do. I was popular, you know." Her voice trailed off into a murmur, but when Holly tried to extract her hand, she asked, "Do you sew?"

"No."

"That's too bad. What do you do? 4-H?"

The girl grinned sourly at Chuck, as if she were making a confession that implicated him. "I'm a cheerleader."

Chuck hated irony. "She's smart," he corrected. "She gets straight A's."

The two women ignored him.

"Oh, honey, if I had eyes, I would teach you. There are so many things . . . " Her voice trailed off again at the

vision of all she might teach or, perhaps, of all she'd forgotten. "We made our own. We were famous for it. I
sewed and put up, and made the cheese and bread and
wine—mulberry wine, from off the tree out back. And
Charlie, he could work magic with wood. You've seen the
barn. He built that, he and his two cousins. Built the walls
on the ground. Then the neighbors came with horses to
help lift up the pieces, and they took all the credit."

Chuck shoved his hands into his pockets. There wasn't
a mulberry tree within twenty miles that he knew of, and
the barn, if the long warehouse-looking building where
the hogs were penned could be called a barn, had been
built by a contractor from Bloomington.

Holding Holly's hand tight to her bosom, Grandma
seemed for all the world to be sounding the girl's eyes.

"Have you seen Charlie?"

"No, Nana."

The old woman shook her head. "He wasn't much to
look at." Then, abruptly, she seemed full of eagerness.
"Chuck! You know the picture albums upstairs?"

Chuck knew all about them. He used to spend hours
searching out the grandparents he'd never known; pon-
dering men gathered around a steam thresher; contemplating a little girl, all knees and starch, holding a rabbit
kit up to the lens; and wondering what claim those pre-
served half seconds had on him.

"You don't mind?" Granny asked the girl. "Some people hate looking at that old stuff."

"I'd love it."

The old woman turned to where she thought the boy
would be and addressed the organ. "You take her upstairs and show her those pictures. Show her my wedding
photos—I made that dress myself, every stitch of it, with
material that came from Chicago."

There was a slyness in her smile that Chuck didn't like.

"We've got to take care of you, Granny."

"Oh, pshaw! I've got my ball game. Tie me down if you want, I'm not going anywhere."

He would have said, "Another time," but Holly had already reset the earphones on Grandma's head.

She held out her hand for his. "I want to see the folks your dad thinks are so much better than mine."

"Now, here's the first half recap, brought to you by State Farm Insurance and your local State Farm agent. Like a good neighbor, State Farm is there. Rebounding seemed to be the name of the game in the first half. Griffin took an early 6–2 lead on three straight rebound baskets by all-state forward Jimmy Williams. . . . "

Granny counted fifty before she lifted the earphones from her head.

"Chuck?"

Her hands trembling, she felt alongside the chair for her walker, drew it to the front, hooked the strap of her purse around one of its uprights, and gradually, her arms vibrating from the strain, lifted herself up. Feeling her knees lock beneath her, she paused to let the dizziness evaporate.

Holly had never seen a room like it—certainly not in her house, with its cheap shag carpets and plush-upholstered chairs, where even the dining room table could be broken down for a move—but she was not sure she liked it any better. Too much wood, too many shades of brown. The floor was thick-slatted and cracked, darker near the walls than it was in the middle. A huge blond desk had been jammed up next to the door, and a skinny reddish chair squatted under it like a very thin man trying to milk a large cow. Next to it was a dresser, rounded at the corners and made out of, at least, three different colors of wood, supporting an egg-shaped mirror bordered in leaves. Jammed into the remaining wall space were an

ordinary pine bureau, a walnut bookcase filled with hard-
backs whose titles had worn away and yellowing paper-
back crosswords, and a nightstand with a porcelain basin
and pitcher on top. The four-poster was right out of Count
Dracula, the wood stained so dark it was almost black,
with a white chenille bedspread, tassled along the hem.
It had a canopy with a carved frame from which bunches
of grapes hung like wooden icicles from a border of
leaves, with a lacy white backing showing through in between. There was no sense of balance. No one had cared
to coordinate the effect the way she had learned in home
ec. It was more like an antique shop, she decided, than a
room to live in. While Chuck knelt and opened the cabinet door of the nightstand, Holly tried to imagine each
piece in a room designed by someone, like herself, who
knew what she was doing. She retreated a few steps and
tried to sit on the edge of the bed, but it swallowed her
and, in the next instant, dropped her on the floor.

Chuck didn't bother to look around, but his back was
shaking.

"It's not funny! How was I supposed to know there's no
stuffing?"

"Feathers, spacehead. Haven't you ever sat on a
feather bed?"

She got up and tested the mattress with her hand.
"Wow!" Then she threw herself as far under the canopy
as she could. The mattress swelled up around her. "This
is great!"

Chuck went on pulling albums out of the nightstand.
Folding her legs underneath her Indian-style, Holly
glanced around again. The room looked different from
here, with the ceiling cut off by the canopy and the lace
and icicles hanging down, prettier and more threatening
than before. The weird hodgepodge of furniture seemed
to halfway make sense. She could see patterns in the
wood. Not patterns like the ones in a skyline, but like

those on the rock sides of the gravel pit they used to swim in before her father ran off, where you could have sworn that the rock and the water were moving together.

"We'd better look at these downstairs," Chuck said. "I don't trust her alone."

Once she saw those patterns, the room seemed to grow larger and vibrate—dark to light, light to dark again—in one pulsating organ chord of brown that echoed through her body. And there he was, blinking down at her with three black-leaved albums in his arms. Her fingers skimmed in circles where the mattress swelled beside her.

She thought it over, pushing her tongue between the gap in her front teeth, following the way her fingers smoothed and roughened the nap of the spread, and smiled. "It's pretty."

Boiling water.

Granny took the pan from its hook on the pegboard, covered the bottom with water, and turned on the electric range one notch to high. Then she stopped, momentarily baffled. It had been so long since she'd done any work she'd lost the knack of thinking, What next?

She remembered her purse, dredged it up, poured its contents onto the counter, and made a quick inventory: eight hard-as-rocks chunks of fudge chocolate, slips of paper, lint, a handful of cashew nuts, a pencil, a key.

She tried biting into the candy. It was too hard. She felt their hands picking at her as she lay on the floor, the tablecloth in her arms. Damn them!

If she'd been sitting, she would have given up, but since she was standing, there was nothing to do but go on. The dizziness returned. She had to remember to breathe. In her excitement, every time she thought, What next? she held her breath.

She took a knife and cut into the fudge. Some of them

were still soft inside. She prayed God the chocolate would melt. Her hand over the saucepan told her the water had come to a boil. She dropped in several pieces, burning her fingers on the edge. Sweat trickled down her face. Never, since she had given up her apartment in Danvers, had she done so much so fast (she could see the apartment clearly—the blistered paint on the bathroom ceiling, the smoke alarm in the hall that went off every time she cooked, the long couch in the living room where she often slept).

Ice cream.

She hadn't thought to check. In the freezer her hand fell at once on a box. She took it out, tasted it. Chocolate. It would do.

She leaned against the counter, spinning—shadow to light, light to shadow. When she woke, she had to push back memories that were crowding to the surface, trying to drag her down.

Hurrying over to the pan, she dipped in her spoon. Nothing there. She swished it around. Nothing.

"Arthur?"

No one answered.

Then she realized what had happened. The fudge had melted.

Chuck's stomach felt queasy. Standing there, holding her jeans by one of the legs, he watched as she sat back, cross-legged, calmly removing her bra and tossing it onto the floor. He let the jeans drop. This was a mistake. The heaviness that had come over him like a premonition when things were about to go wrong weighed on him. He could taste humiliation, even as he pulled off his T-shirt. There she was with only her panties on, chewing at her lower lip, and this time it was real. His belly had knotted so tight, he didn't even have a hard-on. He stripped off his own pants and was half into bed, his hand on her thigh, when he realized he'd forgotten something and went back for the rubber.

"Forgot." He tried to smile, but her face had changed.

"How long have you had that?"

"A while."

She frowned like a judge. He had known this was a mistake, now he knew its dimensions. In one second she had seen the anger, the violent dreams, the devious motives, the secret masturbation, and she hated him.

"Let me see."

He tore open the prophylactic seal and handed it to her. She held the rubber between the tips of her fingernails like something dead.

"Yech! It's got stuff on it."

"Lubricant," he said. "So it won't hurt."

Holly unrolled the condom. Perversely, as though his prick felt a sympathy for its thin plastic image, he got hard. She jiggled it, let it swing around, then tore it in half and threw it in his face.

"I don't want that thing in me."

"Holly! Dammit, look at me!" She was rubbing her hands furiously on the bedspread. "You stupid bitch, this is supposed to protect you!"

"I don't want to be protected."

Her eyes, when they confronted him, flickered with anger. "You still want to?"

In his relief that maybe she did not hate him, he thought: I love you. He thought: I'm sorry. But what he said was, "Yes."

She allowed him a little grimace of a grin. "Then take your socks off."

"Why?"

"Because they're gross!" This time the grin was real.

Grumbling, he turned to climb out and smacked his head against the canopy frame. "Shit! Christ Almighty!"

She burst out laughing, holding her head and rocking on the mattress as if she were the one in pain.

"Bitch!"

He made a grab at her, but she rolled away, shrieking. When he went after her, the down shifted like sand under his knees.

"You're so clumsy!" Tears streamed down her cheeks and dribbled from her nose.

He got her hand and part of a leg, but she pushed him away, and he fell back, sinking into the mattress, and then Holly was on top of him laughing. She wiped her nose with the back of her hand and kissed the red mark on his forehead.

"Poor Chuckie."

It was finished. Granny had carved chips of ice cream from the box, covered them with cashews, and poured so much fudge over them that the sauce had dripped over the edge. She had shuffled from the counter to the table without her walker, so pleased with herself that when she put down the bowl she nearly upended it. Now she sat before her creation, struck by her accomplishment— even more by the marvelous mischief of it. They would say she was senile. They would hire more guards and give them rope, because in spite of the odds, she had stolen something back from them. It seemed almost sacrilege to lift the spoon.

But the aroma of fudge would not allow her abstract victories. It spoke quite plainly to her nerves and said, "Now."

The first bite disappointed her—all ice cream. She tongued the lump from one side of her mouth to the other until it dissolved. Since she hadn't eaten anything rich in so long, it felt heavy and strange. Only after she'd swallowed did something like a taste come to her senses, more flowery than sweet. In the next mouthful she got some fudge, but barely enough to tell the difference. The unfamiliar sweetness made her jaws ache as if she were sucking a lemon, but this time the ice cream had settled more lightly on her tongue and she could taste it.

Finally she found the knack again, dragging the edge for a nut, then scooping into the fudge and tunneling up through the cream. She began to eat more quickly, no longer savoring each sensation; and the more she ate, the more her appetite increased. Even without isolating them, she knew all the flavors: oil and salt, cream and lye, flowers and musk, and under them the dark taste, sticking to her dentures like tar, of earth and honey.

Soon, though, the euphoria dissolved into uneasiness. Her stomach rebelled against so much at once. She had to set down the spoon and grip the edge of the table to force back surges of nausea. When they receded, she held on, mouth wide, laboring for breath, under the impression that some force was trying to drag her from the chair. Her head throbbed. She thought, What next?

When she had control of herself again, she continued eating her sundae, though the ice cream had puddled and every bite she took tasted partly of bile. The past surfaced once more, and this time she did not care to check it.

She could almost hear him, at first, going one-two-one-two the way his sister had taught him in the parlor. But once he'd gotten a sense of her body, Charlie stopped treating her arm like a pump handle, and they spun easily in time with the others around the great fire. The older couples dropped out, one after the other, but the younger stayed. And poor Paul Kammerer, whom none of them could hear, folded and unfolded his accordion like a fan. Round and round they spun, fire to shadow, shadow to fire, and the stamp of their feet on the hard earth set the music. After a while she could feel Charlie swinging wide, and she lifted her chin, daring him. Out of the circle they

spun, across the yard and all the way down the lane to
the road. Later, more slowly, they danced their way back.

She hurt everywhere. The pain, rising from her stomach, spread across her shoulders and into her arms and
back. She sat stock-still, listening to a vague sound like
the footfalls of an animal at night, and followed their
progress. She shivered, and that hurt, too. The pain ad-
vanced; it knotted the muscles of her back and throbbed
in her fingers. The gray shadows rushed by. Her feet were
cold, her lips were cold, her eyes burned like tiny fires
set in caves of ice. (In the lot of the Texaco station in
Danvers, the crushed remains of a car. A group of teenagers stood around it.)

Then she couldn't tell where the pain was or when her
breath came and went, but her heart was making a terrible racket in her ears. With every nerve singing, she
could no longer feel pain as pain. It was like the rush of a
wind around her body. Looking up, she saw that the
clouds were caught in the trees.

The sky began to fill with fire, flashes of color mixing
and jostling like children with no rhyme or reason. There
was a rhythm, of sorts, to their comings and goings, and
it seemed to her that there were shapes in the flames.
She knew they were real because she could feel their
motion inside her. The sky came slowly closer. She
reached for it.

"God, how beautiful!"

The noise in her ears ceased. A small white spot appeared in the sky, grew like the sun when she looked at
it straight until it covered the trees and the land. Her
body was clothed in white, and for the first time since
Charlie died, she felt warm.

"Are you sure?" Holly demanded.

He looked up angrily from where the old woman lay on
the floor. "You want to try?"

"I believe you."

Granny was dead. The girl had never seen anyone dead before—it looked ridiculous. She knew she was supposed to feel sad or scared, but what she really felt was embarrassed—and worried that Chuck would blame her. He took off the corpse's glasses and tried to close its eyes with the flat of his hand the way they did in the movies, but they wouldn't shut. He dropped the glasses, and it took him several tries to retrieve them.

"You want me to clean up?" It was the only way she could think of to say, Don't worry. I'll help.

"I don't know. Maybe we shouldn't."

"Why? They don't need to know everything."

She wasn't sure she liked the relief he seemed to find in that, but she began to clear away the debris. The old woman had left an incredible mess—a half-overturned pan, an ice-cream box wallowing in a puddle of chocolate milk, chocolate on the floor, the range, the table. Holly deposited the box, the contents of the pan, and what she could scrape from various places into a plastic freezer bag. Meanwhile Chuck paced next to the body, muttering the same thing over and over in different words.

"She planned it. . . . She tricked us. . . . She wanted to kill herself.

"Everybody will know. They'll say it's our fault, they'll say we helped her. My parents will blame you. They'll keep us apart. If you think my father's bad, you should see my mother when she gets going. And Uncle Art . . . " The contemplation of what Arthur might do silenced him for a moment, until he discovered he'd been tracking chocolate all over the floor. "Jesus. If she wanted to kill herself, why didn't she eat a Hershey bar?"

She kissed him. "Don't be stupid." And handed him the plastic sack. "Make yourself useful. Take this out to the trash."

While he was gone, Holly paused to think how odd it was that dead, with her glasses off, Granny Frisch looked

so much younger and stronger. She imagined herself
dead and shivered, repulsing the image. In its place came
the consciousness that they were caught. The idea didn't
trouble her as much as she expected it to. Having to own
up and pay the consequences wouldn't change what
they'd done. Lies changed things, she knew, even the
things you didn't lie about. She'd seen her mother
change. Yet she went on scraping burnt chocolate from
the bottom of the pan.

Chuck came back, brushing himself off. "It's snowing."

She tossed him a sponge.

The body swung awkwardly as they lugged it to the
couch, not heavy but so ungainly that the girl kept having
to catch her grip. The still-warm flesh raised goose bumps
on her arms. The moment she'd touched it, her sympathy
had disappeared. Like Chuck, she wished the lady had
bothered to think about what she was leaving behind for
them. As they eased the body down and adjusted the
cushions, Holly smelled shit. Repelled, she backed away,
hands out from her sides, and from that distance, glared
at the corpse with something approaching hatred.

A tinny chorus sang from the headphones:

> Dashing through the snow
> In a one-horse open sleigh
> O'er the fields we go
> Laughing all the way. . . .

She punched the receiver's power button.

Chuck must have smelled it, too. He took off his sweatshirt and spread it under the old woman's butt.

She picked up the headphones and put them on the
mantel, noticed the baseball cap and picked that up also.
Weighing it with one finger, she looked out past the reflection of her boyfriend arranging the dead woman's
feet, past the lane and the snow-dusted field to the high-

way, where the snow fell straight down through cones of light.

"Try it on," he said.

When a car drove through, she noticed, the flurry seemed to bend in toward it, as if the snow were trying to force its way through the windshield.

She dropped the hat in a chair. "That's not funny."

He didn't answer. She watched him glance at the clock, shove his hands into his pockets. Instead of going over to her, he sat in the lounge chair, with his hands in his pockets, and stared out the window. She felt deserted. Why didn't he hold her or say something that would comfort her?

"We're going to catch hell," he said.

"So what?"

If he heard the accusation in her voice, he didn't say anything, just patted the arm of the chair. Reluctantly she wandered over and sat on it, leaning away from him.

Chuck laid his hand on her thigh. The distances had disappeared, and after the first shock, so had the guilt and disgust he'd felt about Grandma Frisch. They had been replaced by a lassitude that seemed almost like a sense of humor. It would be great if Holly were right, he thought, that whatever his parents tried to do wouldn't matter, but she didn't have his family.

The warmth of her thigh aroused a comfortable sensuality, under whose influence he wanted to hold her and stay at arm's length at the same time. He felt completed but also, in a way, as if he'd used her up.

"Look at the snow."

She looked, but what she saw was the slough, angling across the fields like a black scar. "I hate snow."

He tried to take her hand, but she wouldn't let him have it.

"Why?"

From the flatness in his voice, she decided he really

didn't give a damn. "Something that happened at Trinity."

The scar resolved into the reflection of the body on the couch, and without warning the stupidness and ugliness broke in on her, and she flew at him with both fists as hard as she could.

"Damn it! Goddamn it!"

He caught both arms and held them tight.

"Goddamn you, too!"

He kept holding her, silently appraising her, until she relaxed and sat back.

She wondered what he thought of her now, decided that she didn't want to know, and impulsively kissed his ear.

"What happened at Trinity?"

"Sister Bonaventura . . . Why do you want to know?"

He thought, Because I love you. But he said, "I've got this faceful of bruises."

"Serves you right." She studied their reflection in the window. "I was nine or so, and in religion class one of the nuns was doing the Ten Commandments—you know, Honor your father and mother? That was when my father was still around. I asked her, what happens if my father tells me to break one of the Commandments? Do I have to obey? I think I asked if it was mortal or venial. She got real upset and wanted to know what he'd done, and I said he hadn't done anything. I was just curious.

"Sister came charging down the row, screaming about Satan and dirty-minded little girls, pulled me up by the hair, and dragged me to the window and made me look at the snow. 'You see that?' she said. 'Every flake is a soul in torment, falling into hell. Every soul crying out for mercy, but God will not listen. Do you know why? Because they questioned His law!' "

He stroked her hair. "That's sick."

The snow was coming down a little heavier now, and of

course, it was beautiful. She wished it weren't. It would
be so much easier if only the things she loved were beautiful.

"They wouldn't let me stay."

"Who?"

"After school." But Chuck didn't get it. "The snow was
still falling, but they wouldn't let me stay. I had to run
home through it." She could feel them even now, the
souls of the dead, melting on her skin and running down
her face like tears.

He embraced her, tightly, as much to console himself
as to comfort her, feeling an echo of the nun's God-
sickness in himself.

For a while they said nothing. She understood that he
was moved and didn't know how to go on, so she asked,
knowing he still believed, "Do you think it's a sin, what
we did?"

He seemed to turn it over in his mind. "Probably."

"Do you mind?"

"No."

Holly glanced at the old woman on the couch and felt a
peculiar affection. "Do you think she knew?"

"Grandma? Come on. She was just hoping we'd stay up
there with her pictures." He let out a long sigh. "They're
going to hate us."

Let them, she thought, nuzzling his shoulder. "I don't
think they'll do anything to us. Your mother can't even
look me in the eye."

"But she sees you. What she doesn't look at, those are
the things she sees best. Hey, if Aunt Ellen tells her what
we were doing up there, she'll look at you. Talk to you,
too."

"She can talk to my mother. They deserve each other."
She liked the idea of the two of them bitching over her,
and liked her mother better for the idea.

Chuck patted her thigh—the way he'd patted the arm

of the chair, she thought. "We could tell them she died in the chair."

Holly hunched around until her back was to him. "It wouldn't work."

"Worth a try." He sounded pleased with himself.

"No, it's not."

The snowstorm had stopped quite suddenly when Holly wasn't looking. Through their reflection in the window, the land stretched out, a patchwork of gray-black shapes broken on one side by the long curve of the highway. The sky was darker here than in town, and the trees blacker. It comforted her, somehow, that she couldn't tell where the fields ended and the sky began.

"There's Arthur!" She could feel Chuck's body tense. "You can't miss those beams."

Holly could see them approach the overhead exit sign on the interstate—two pairs of headlights, one white and one yellow. The truck behind them vanished and reappeared as it passed under the cones of light.

The old woman's mouth had fallen open. She looked as if she were talking to someone on the ceiling.

Taking both his large hands in hers, Holly pressed them to her belly and watched the truck slowly making its way against the drifting snow until it passed beyond the window frame.